P9-CQO-447

BURNOUT

ALSO BY ADRIENNE MARIA VRETTOS

Sight
Skin
The Exile of Gigi Lane

BURNOUT

ADRIENNE MARIA VRETTOS

MARGARET K. McELDERRY BOOKS

New York London Toronto Sydney

MARGARET K. McELDERRY BOOKS

An imprint of Simon & Schuster Children's Publishing Division

1230 Avenue of the Americas, New York, New York 10020

MARGARET K. MCELDERRY BOOKS is a trademark of Simon & Schuster, Inc.

For information about special discounts for bulk purchases, please contact Simon & Schuster Special Sales at 1-866-506-1949 or business@simonandschuster.com.

The Simon & Schuster Speakers Bureau can bring authors to your live event. For more information or to book an event, contact the Simon & Schuster Speakers Bureau at 1-866-248-3049 or visit our website at www.simonspeakers.com.

Book design by Irene Metaxatos

The text for this book is set in Adobe Caslon.

Manufactured in the United States of America

10 9 8 7 6 5 4 3 2 1

Library of Congress Cataloging-in-Publication Data

Vrettos, Adrienne Maria.

Burnout / Adrienne Maria Vrettos.—1st ed.

p. cm.

Summary: Months after coming out of alcohol and drug rehab, high school student Nan wakes up on the subway the day after Halloween wearing a torn Halloween costume, her long hair cut, and "HELP ME" scrawled across her chest, feeling sick and having no idea how she got there.

ISBN 978-1-4169-9469-5 (hardcover)

ISBN 978-1-4391-6312-2 (eBook)

[1. Drug abuse—Fiction. 2. Alcoholism—Fiction. 3. Emotional problems—Fiction. 4. New York (N.Y.)—Fiction.] I. Title.

PZ7.V9855Bu 2011

[Fic]—dc22

2010051617

FIRST EDITION

FOR JEFF, FOR WREN,
AND FOR DEZ

BURNOUT

PROLOGUE

This is a ghost story.
I am the ghost.

TODAY

I wake up falling. I am falling fast, away from myself, but when my body should slap against the ground, it isn't the ground at all, but black water that swallows me whole, and the last thing I see is my own face staring up at me before the water sucks me down.

I have the weirdest dreams when I'm sober.

I wake up listening. I hear the Tick come into my bedroom, and I know when I open my eyes, I am going to see him kneeling by my bed, wearing his Halloween vampire teeth and smelling like little-boy sleep, wet-lipped with stifled laughter, waiting for me to wake up and pour him a bowl of Cap'n Crunch for breakfast. He will poke me and whisper, "Nan, are you dead again?"

I wake up freezing, and now I am getting tired of this and want to wake up for real. This dream isn't even a dream; it's a memory in the shape of a dream. I am at the deep end of a drained pool in Connecticut. It's early spring, and I am freezing. I've slept on a long patio-chair cushion covered with flowers the color of orange sorbet. There's a matching cushion on top of me; a stiff, unforgiving blanket. I blink my eyes against the too-bright sky. It smells like dead leaves and cold and something else. My feet lie in an ice-crusted black soup of rotting things. I roll over on my side and try to throw up, but there's nothing in my stomach. From the look of the mess next to me, I lost it all last night.

I will never, ever drink again.

I think I might still be drunk.

Nan! Seemy yells, laughing, from over the side of the pool. She's wearing a Santa hat that's too big for her little pixie head. *What the hell! Patrick told you to sleep in his sister's room!*

I push the cushion off and sit up. What feels like a tsunami-size wave of dizziness crashes over me, and I close my eyes before it can flip me upside down and drown me. When I open my eyes I am staring at my hands in my lap. They are red with cold, except for my knuckles, which are chapped and white.

Nan! Seemy yells again, not laughing this time.

Who's Patrick? I finally ask, pulling my feet out of the water and shaking them off.

I am.

I look up, and the kid is vaguely familiar, with the sort of stupid face Seemy always falls for. *Ugh,* I groan aloud when I recognize him. *That kid?* I remember him from last night, this douchy kid from the suburbs that Seemy insisted we bring back to the carriage house. She threw a freaking tantrum when Toad and I, in a rare moment of agreement, told her the carriage house was supposed to be just for us. The three of us argued about it while Patrick waited across the street, trying not to look alarmed at the fact that his hook-up location was being decided by committee. It ended with Seemy getting her way because she said, *Fine, me and him will just go someplace else,* which was shocking because I don't think Toad or I ever considered that her leaving was even an option. The fear of her just walking away felt silver and sharp, with a blade that was bigger than my body could take. So we all went to the carriage house. We climbed the iron gate and then rubbed the rust off on our pants as we stole across the muddy lawn in the dark. We turned sideways to squeeze between the barn-style wooden doors. I hoped Patrick would get stuck and then hated him for slipping through so easily. Work on the place had stopped before they even tore out the stalls, and the three of us had set up a little living room in the one that stunk the least. That's where Toad and I went, to sit on milk crates and turn on the battery-operated lamp we'd stolen from Eastern Mountain Sports. We made Seemy leave us the bottle of vodka mixed with orange juice before she and Patrick climbed up the ladder to the hayloft. It was just Toad and I downstairs, and he turned on some music, which was good because Toad and I hate each other and I didn't want to have to talk to him. The floor upstairs creaked and he and I avoided looking at each other. Then, even though the music was on, we heard Seemy moan really loud and then laugh, and Toad stood up so fast he knocked over the milk crate. *I'm going,* he said. *Stay and listen if you want.* He turned off the music. *There, now you can hear even better.* I watched him slip between the doors into the night and wondered what I should do. I wished I wasn't so drunk. I wished I could just stand up and walk out and go home, but I knew I wouldn't because that would mean leaving Seemy with some douchy kid from the suburbs. A couple minutes later Seemy called down from the hayloft that it was too cold and Patrick's parents were away for the weekend, and that's how I ended up in the bottom of a drained pool in Connecticut.

And now Patrick is looking down at me, sick with panic. *My parents and sister are coming home early. You guys have to leave,* he says. I keep sitting, keep looking around me, wondering where I put my stuff. *Seriously*, Patrick calls down, *you guys have to leave.*

I sigh. *Fine.*

Patrick and Seemy look into each other's eyes, blush, look down at their shoes. Then Seemy moves her head a little so she catches his gaze, lifts his chin with the tip of her pointer finger. They kiss. Seemy does that little moaning sound in her throat that drives the boys wild. I think maybe they can feel the vibrations on their tongues.

I climb out of the pool. The aluminum ladder is breaking away from the side, so with every step it pulls back, letting loose a spray of cement that rattles down to the bottom. *Let's go,* I say, looking away as they kiss again.

See ya, Patrick says to me.

I say, *I just have to get my stuff.*

His face changes. I see Seemy already has her bag. *You have to go over the fence,* he says, pointing to the white picket fence that lines the far side of the backyard. Between us and the fence there's a football field's worth of brown lawn, which I imagine magically turns into a lush green carpet with the *ch-ch-ch* sprinkler sound of springtime in the suburbs. There's a pool house, which, if I had a brain in my head, I would have slept in. Patrick nudges me, keeps pointing. *Just climb over the fence. That's all you have to do. Just climb the fricking fence, okay?*

I run my hand through my knotted hair, pull my long, multicolored mane over my shoulder, hold out the ends and study the stripes of pink and green. *I need to get my stuff inside*, I say again, waiting a moment before I level my gaze at him. I tower over him. He has to look up. His mouth twists a little. *What?* I tease. *You don't want your parents to meet me?* He shrugs. I clack my tongue ring against my lip ring a few times, grinning as he flinches.

There's a cold gust of wind, and I don't want to be standing here anymore in wet boots, with vomit breath and a crick in my neck. My anger feels liquid and hot, gushing into my lungs like water, billowing and blooming like black roses. I hate Seemy for dragging me out here with her last night and hate myself for coming. We both knew I wouldn't let her go alone.

Come on, Nan, Seemy says, *let's just go.*

I look at her. *Are you kidding? Seemy, how am I going to get on the train? My wallet's inside. My phone. I can't. I need my stuff.*

But she keeps pushing me. *He'll send it to you*, she says.

Yes, yes, he assures me, *I'll send it to the address on the license.*

I'm not from the suburbs, I snap. *I'm a New Yorker. I don't have a license.* I'm embarrassing Seemy, adding an unfortunate postscript to her hookup. Patrick goes really pale, and I see him looking over my shoulder, to the driveway, where a car is slowing.

He yells, *Go!* And Seemy gets pissed because he won't kiss her good-bye, and then she and I are climbing over the white picket fence. These suburban assholes can't built a fence for shit because as soon as I start climbing, the thing starts creaking and leaning, and by the time we're to the top it's almost flat on the ground. Before I run after Seemy, I jump on the fence a couple times to make sure it's good and busted and Seemy is calling back to me, *Jesus, chill out, Nan, I'll buy your stupid train ticket!* And then we're running down this random street flanked by the sort of houses you see in real estate commercials, and my boots are chafing my skin and I think I might get sick again.

At first, when Seemy sees that I'm turning around and jogging toward Patrick's driveway, she chases me, tries to grab my hair to stop me. *He'll get in trouble! Nan! Seriously!* But then she stops chasing me and hides behind one of the neighbors' trash cans and waits for me while I ring Patrick's doorbell and tell his mom, who has the stupid face he does, that I left my stuff inside.

I go back to get Seemy a couple minutes later. She's still crouching behind the trash can, and she looks up at me like she could kill me. *What the hell, Nan?* she says. *You probably got him in so much trouble!*

What do you care? I ask. *You're never going to see him again.*

She shrugs and stands up, crossing her arms. *Whatever.*

I start walking.

Where are you going? she calls after me.

I turn around, keep walking backward. *Train station. Where do you think?*

That's, like, a mile away, she whines. *It's freezing!*

What were you planning on doing?

She shrugs again. *I could call Toad, see if he can borrow a car and come get us.*

I stop walking. *Seemy, that's just cruel.*

She tries to hide her smile. *What?*

The guy's obviously in lust with you, and you're going to make him find a car, drive to Connecticut, and pick you up from your one-night stand?

Seemy laughs. *Maybe? He'd do it.* She looks at me, and I know what she's thinking. She's thinking I'd do it too. She's thinking if she called me and asked me to find a way to Connecticut, I'd get my dad to drive out here in his truck and pick her up.

Just because he would do it doesn't make you any less of an asshole, I tell her.

Fine, she snaps. *We'll walk.*

And we do.

I buy a travel toothbrush set from a vending machine at the train station and use the whole mini tube of toothpaste trying to brush the vileness out of my mouth in the bathroom. There's a cafe at the train station but it's closed because it's Sunday, so we're left shivering on the platform with vending machine Cokes and Doritos for breakfast. Seemy ignores me. I pretend not to care. I pretend that I'm ignoring her too, even though I'm really waiting for her to stop looking right through me as she looks down the track for the train. I hate it when Seemy's mad at me. It makes me wish I could fly away from myself, away from this body that is an open sore for her salted anger, this body that changes without her love. But I can't fly away. I stand next to her and grow larger and uglier and stupider every minute she ignores me. It is good she's not looking at me. I don't want her to see what I really am when I'm not disguised by her friendship. At moments like this it seems inconceivable that she is the same person who presented me with a little homemade book with a hand-sewn binding called *My Friend Nan* on my birthday, or who wiped away my tears and hugged me when I cried about not knowing who my real dad is, or who told me I wasn't really all that big.

I'm not even sure if she's going to sit next to me, but she does, and she puts on her headphones right away so I put on mine. I peel off my boots and wet socks and slip my gloves on my feet to keep them warm. I sit cross-legged, my feet finally warming under the heat of my thighs, and I don't care that my knee is practically in Seemy's lap. We don't talk the whole way back to the city. We're just pulling into the dark underground tunnels that lead to Grand Central station when I feel her tapping on my knee. I look away from my reflection in the now-dark window and see her smiling at me, her fingers working out the rhythm of whatever song she's listening to. I pull off my headphones, thinking she wants to talk. She leaves her headphones on but says too loudly, *I'm sorry I dragged you to Connecticut, Nanja. I was thinking with my quivering loins, not my brain.* I say, *It's okay,* but now she's got her eyes closed, and she's doing this dance in her seat to the music. She takes her fingers away from my knee.

What I want to say to her is, *I love you,* but I know she'd just laugh and say, *I know, I love you too, Nanja.* In the beginning we'd crack each other up, dramatically confessing our love for each other. Yelling out from across the street, *You complete me, Samantha "Seemy" Turbin!* Or from the window of a taxi as it pulled away from my apartment, *Wait for me, Nanja! Wait for me forever.*

But then it wasn't funny anymore to yell it; it kind of made me sick to my stomach because I got scared I meant it in a way she didn't.

In this dream, in this memory, I miss Seemy the way I did when we first stopped hanging out, in that way that hurts the place where your heart and throat touch. My fingers twitch as I count the months since I've seen her. One, two, three, four, five, six. Almost six months. It hurts too much. So I make myself fall back asleep.

I wake up watching. There is a coffee cup on its side under a subway seat. The cup is from Dunkin' Donuts, and most of the coffee has spilled out into a puddle the shape of a flattened frog. *Oh man*, I think, *all that coffee. And it looks nice and creamy, too. Probably lots of sugar. Someone's good morning, just dumped out. That sucks.*

I close my eyes; wait to leave the dream, to fall back into inky blackness, to come out the other side. I open my eyes. The coffee cup is still there. So's the spilled coffee. I close my eyes again. Open. Same thing.

Wait.

I am not asleep. I am not dreaming. I am awake.

Fear flickers electric and hot from the top of my head to the soft soles of my feet. I can almost smell myself burning.

I am not where I'm supposed to be.

My heart is rick-tick-ticking inside my chest, rattling a bone-thunk alarm against my ribs, *Danger, danger, danger.*

And then there is a feeling that tastes bitter on the back of my tongue and makes my blood freeze in my veins, a feeling that makes me want to scream because it fills me with such familiar doubt.

What have I done?

TODAY

There must have been an accident on the subway. I think we must have crashed. Terrible things like that happen here. And then we all forget that they do, until something terrible happens again. A subway crash. That's why I'm lying on my stomach. That's why I hurt so much.

I just wish I knew why nobody is screaming. Don't people usually scream when something terrible happens? Maybe they *are* screaming. Maybe I've hit my head and gone deaf. But then I realize I can hear the hum of the ventilation system.

My face is turned to the side. My right arm hangs off

the seat, palm-up on the floor. I stare at it. I close my eyes again and listen to myself breathing for a while. It calms me down. I open my eyes, look around the car, and see it's empty.

No bloodied bodies.

No twisted wreckage.

No memory.

I'm not supposed to wake up in places like this anymore, not knowing where I've been or what I've done. Blacked out.

No. I *don't* wake up in places like this anymore. I'm different now. I've changed.

When the recorded voice comes over the intercom, it's like my body tries to jump, but it's frozen in place, stuck inside itself, so it feels like every muscle is wrenched, twisted, torn.

"This is the last stop on this train. Please leave the train."

I recognize that announcement. I know where I am. I'm on the L train, and this is the last stop in Manhattan. Everyone's gotten off, and soon a whole other bunch of people will get on. *Just wait*, I tell myself, *somebody's going to come. Somebody's going to help.* I'll tell them . . . what will I tell them? I will say, *Please help me, I'm having an emergency.*

I manage to lift my head a few inches. The skin on my face

sticks to the plastic seat, peels away slowly. I look at the seat. There's a white splotch on the plastic where my cheek was.

I don't understand.

I want to sit all the way up, but my brain starts spinning one way, and my skull starts spinning another, so I lay my head down and close my eyes and fall back asleep.

I wake up because my right arm has that prickly pins-and-needles feeling. I stare at my hand on the floor, wiggle my fingers, pull up my arm so it's next to me on the seat. It feels heavy and dark and thick. I keep it next to me, letting the blood work its way through.

I hear a noise at the far end of the subway car, and I move my eyes to see the door between the cars open and the train conductor walk through. There's a pause in his step when he sees me, and he watches me as he walks closer.

I'm embarrassed to be lying down, so I push myself up, until I'm posed like a beached mermaid, still on my stomach, my legs stretched out on the bench. And then things go dark, like someone has switched off a light to the world. Just for a moment, just long enough for me to feel like I'm falling backward.

"You all right?" the MTA guy asks. He is in front of me now. He has a graying mustache, and it twitches when he speaks.

"Something happened to me, but I don't remember . . ."

I try to finish, but it comes out a dry croak. I swallow. My throat hurts so much that tears spring to my eyes, but my face is numb, I can't feel them slide down my cheeks.

He nods, like my tears have answered his question. "It's okay, let me go call for help. Why don't you lie back down?"

I shake my head, clear my throat, ignore the pain, and say, "I want to sit up."

I roll over, sit up, and keep my legs on the bench because they're too heavy to move. My arms are limp beside me, and for a moment I can't lift my head from where it lolls on my chest and I can't breathe and I'm going to suffocate and die right here and it's just such bullshit, to die like this, without being able to fight and without anyone knowing how much I love them and how sorry I am for the things I've done. But then my neck muscles work, and I can lift my head from my chest and breathe again.

The guy unzips his blue MTA jacket and takes it off, holds it out. I start to wave him away. Four deep cuts curve their way from the inside of my left elbow to my wrist. They are dark with new scabs, and as soon as I look at them, I'm suddenly aware how much they sting.

"What happened to my arm?" I whisper, holding it out for him to see. My voice is raspy; my tongue feels thick, too big for my mouth.

"I'm not sure, miss." He stares at my arm, his nostrils flare a little. His mustache twitches. He lays the jacket on my lap and walks quickly toward the operating cubby. I let my arm fall to the side, banging my hand on the seat.

"I'm having an emergency," I call after him, but he doesn't turn.

I look down.

No wonder he gave me his jacket.

I'm wearing a dress. It's pink, strapless, and it's cut too low in the boobs and too high in the thighs. There is a tear on the right side where it couldn't hold me in. I think it's made out of plastic. I'm not supposed to describe my body as "burly" because Mom says that's hate speech, but that's what I am. I am a burly girl testing the seams of a too-small plastic dress. I would never wear something like this on purpose. I can feel the train seat on the bare backs of my upper thighs, and my skin crawls. I pull the jacket over me, covering my chest.

The train conductor comes back, hands me a bottle of water.

"This isn't my dress," I croak. I try to open the water, but my hands are shaking. He gently takes it from me, opens it, and hands it back.

"Transit cops will be here in a minute."

The darkness comes again. Three heartbeats long.

When the light comes the MTA guy is waving his hand in front of my eyes and saying, "Oh man." I drink the water. First a sip, and then a gulp, and then I've drained the whole thing. "I feel really weird right now."

He swallows, and nods, takes the empty water bottle from me and sets it on the seat behind him.

I sigh and pull my feet off the bench. They fall to the floor with a *thunk-thunk*. My feet are filthy, all the way up to my calves. Caked with dried mud, tight on my skin, itchy.

"Have you seen my shoes?" I ask.

He shakes his head, hesitates, and then says, "Do you remember what you took?"

I blink at him, pretend not to understand. "I can't find my shoes."

"I know, hon, but you need to remember what you took. The drugs," he says.

The drugs! He said it like he was saying *the boogeyman!* Or *terrorists!*

"I don't do drugs." I say firmly, just like we role-played at New Beginnings. He doesn't understand. "I made a promise. *And* I went to rehab," I assure him. "I'm just having an emergency."

I'm not making sense.

"It's . . . it's going to be all right," the MTA guy says,

trying to sound reassuring. "The cops will call your parents for you."

"My mom's upstate," I tell him. "She's painting at a friend's cabin. She can't come get me." My voice cracks.

It happens again. Darkness crams itself between the seconds and I tumble right in. "Did you say something?" I ask, when the seconds splice themselves back together.

"I said, everything's going to be okay."

"My mom didn't want to leave me alone in the apartment, but I told her she could trust me, and now look what happened."

"I'm sure she'll understand."

"My dad will come first. He's in Greenpoint, but he's not my real dad. He's the Tick's dad. My dad was a sperm donor. But I call the Tick's dad *Dad*, you know? Because he is. Even if we don't live with him."

The MTA guy blinks at me, and I want to stop talking, but I can't.

"I'm clean. Clean as a whistle. They tinkle-test me at school. I leave the sample with the school nurse." It is killing my throat to talk this much, but he doesn't believe me. "Something happened to me," I tell him, "you have to help me. I didn't do this to myself." I hold my arm out again.

"Help is coming. You need to calm down now." I hear a slight hint of a Southern accent.

"You think I'm on drugs?" I ask him.

He manages to shake his head and shrug and sigh all at the same time.

"Is that what you told the cops when you called them?"

"I just told them there was a girl that needed help. That's all."

"Do you think they'll put me away?" I groan. "I bet they try to put me away again. Rehab's no joke, mister, even the one I went to, which was like the neutered version. It's not Nan's Fun-Time Musical Sing-Along, you know. I don't want to go back there. I don't *need* to go back there."

"And you won't go back," he tells me, "because you haven't done anything, right?"

I smirk at him. "You know that's not how it works. I'm a kid." I make a zero shape with my hand and hold it up. "I have zero rights. They'll send me just because I *look* like a screwup, when really I'm just having . . ."

Darkness.

"An emergency?" he asks, and his voice brings things back into the light.

"Right! An emergency."

"I think you're going to be just fine. The cops are going to be here soon."

"The cops," I repeat. "It's all going sideways, isn't it? I

mean, I'm sitting here, suffering from some kind of non-drug-induced amnesia, and my brain is all funny and I'm hearing myself talk and it sounds like somebody else is talking, except it's coming out of my own mouth, you know? And all this is happening and you've called the cops and they're going to put me back in rehab and my mom is going to be so upset and my little brother is going to cry. But I've been trying so hard and I haven't hung out with Seemy in months because I'm not supposed to anymore and I don't hang out with *anyone*. I'm like a self-declared leper. I'm getting Bs this semester, did you know that? So . . . I think I'm just going to go."

The MTA guy stopped paying attention, but now he looks at me. "No, I think you should stay."

"Nah." I stand up, cringing at the pain in my body, and try to smile at the guy. "I'm just going to bail. You've been awesome. Seriously, they should, like, promote you or name a train after you or something."

"The cops are on their way," the guy says, and even though he says it like it's supposed to be reassuring, it sounds like a threat.

"Come on, man," I say, "I'm fine. Really. I've got to get to school. It's Halloween, you know."

"Halloween was last night," he says, shaking his head a little.

"It was?"

He nods.

"Well," I say, "I guess that explains the dress."

A businesswoman steps onto the train, looks at us. The train conductor shakes his head slightly at her, and she steps back off, says something to the other people that were going to board behind her. I watch them in the reflection of the far window, looking in at me as they walk to the next car.

"I'm really just going to . . ." I trail off, catching my reflection in the window behind him. "What happened to me?" I ask, leaning forward to stare at my reflection. My hair is gone, or most of it, anyway. What's left is chopped into short, uneven chunks. And my face is painted like a skeleton. White, with messy black circles around my eyes and mouth. And my eyes. There is something wrong with my eyes. "Ah, hell," I groan. "I'm going to scream now."

TODAY

I scream so loud the MTA guy shoots out his hands like he wants to keep me from screaming myself to pieces. But I jerk sideways, out of his reach, and even though I'm screaming and I'm scared, I think, *You can run now,* and I do.

I go for the open door at the end of the train, but I overshoot it and smash into the end of the car. I grab on to the doorjamb and launch myself out of the subway car and onto the platform, though I don't make it far. I land on the strip of little nubby yellow things that line the edge of the platform, meant to keep people from slipping and falling into the pit and getting creamed by a train.

The nubs dig into the soles of my bare feet, painfully separating all the little bones, until I get to the smooth tiles in the middle of the platform. I slip immediately, crash to my knees, and when I look behind me, I see the MTA guy running out of the train, talking on his radio. There are a bunch of other people on the platform, and some spread out away from me, some step forward like they want to help. I scramble back up and go for the stairs.

My mom says bodies like ours are made for football and slaying dragons.

Dollface, don't you know the big-boned girls are the ones who'll save the world? I don't need my body to save the world, I just need it to save myself, and right now it's doing a piss-poor job. Mom says I shouldn't curse my body, I shouldn't wage a war I can't win, but right now, trying to heave my big-boned glory up these stairs, all I can do is hiss, "Come on!" I am a bear lumbering up a mountain. I am the mountain, too.

I want to shoot like fireworks from the subway station; I want to explode in the air above Manhattan before all of my color sizzles away and I dissolve into nothing. But by the time I see the light of day above me, I am gasping for breath, using the railing to pull myself up one step at a time, my body heavy like wet sand. It is rush hour, so people pushing their way to the surface surround me, and a few of them look back at me after they pass. I want to say, *I'm fine.* I want to say, *Help me.* But I can't breathe, so I don't say anything at all.

I worry the MTA guy is behind me, so when I finally make it out of the subway onto the sidewalk, I force myself to start walking.

Calm down, calm down, calm down, I tell myself, my breath still catching in my throat, tears still streaming down my face no matter how fast I wipe them off. The paint on my skin is so thick I can't even feel my hands on my face. Under my fingertips the paint feels like hard plastic that's been shattered with a thousand hairline fractures, a puzzle that refuses to come apart even though I dig at it with my nails. People look at me in alarm, and I pretend not to notice.

Car tires pull up the confetti carpet from last night's Halloween parade as cars dodge and weave down Sixth Avenue. My bare feet pick up torn bits of papier-mâché, dried Silly String, and other, more organic things I try not to identify. I should figure out where I'm going. I should figure out where I've been. The scar on my forehead itches underneath the face paint, but I can't seem to dig down enough to scratch it, so I rub it with the coarse fabric of the MTA coat sleeve instead.

I want to stop walking now, but I'm afraid to. It feels like if I stop, everything will stop. All the people around me, the cars, the noise, the wind, the world, it will all just stop and everything will fall over like cardboard cutouts and I'll be standing on this freezing cold sidewalk by myself in a city full of dead things.

I keep walking.

I shouldn't have gotten off the subway. That was a "bad choice." That wasn't a "good decision." Dr. Friedman wouldn't approve. She would want to know why. *Why would you get off the subway, Nan? That man was going to help you.* She'd give me that same puzzled look my mom always gave me when she wanted to know why, why, why I did the things I did. And the answer would be the same. *I don't know. I just did them.*

If I had stayed on the subway, the cops would have come. And if the cops had come, they would have asked questions, and I wouldn't have had any answers. And grown-ups hate it when you don't have answers. They'd have brought me to the hospital. They'd have called my mom. *Ma'am, your daughter is an idiot. You'd better come quick.* They'd have poked me and prodded me and tried to make me remember.

What if I don't want to remember?

Why would I want to?

Why would I want to know a story that ends with me waking up half naked with no memory and most of my hair hacked off? That's what people don't understand about blacking out. Most of the time it's for your own good. Why would you want to remember stumbling into Saint Patrick's Cathedral and puking into the holy water in front of a busload of horrified Japanese tourists?

Just for example.

That's the sort of thing that's funny only if someone else is telling the story, telling you what you did, laughing with you about it because it's actually so terrible you think you might cry. That's the sort of thing your best friend and you could laugh so hard over you pee your pants.

But I don't have friends anymore. On purpose. I'm a lone wolf. And I'm stoic. I'm a stoic lone wolf who walks quietly through the halls of her new school, talking to no one. It's better that way. Nobody gets hurt. Especially me.

My stomach hurts. Cramps. Like I ate something bad.

I turn down a side street to puke, and get slapped in the face by a screaming gust of wind. It stops me in my tracks, its chill so sudden and so cold it feels like my body is finally being shocked into wakefulness. The urge to puke is gone.

It is freezing, and it is wonderful. It feels like it knocks the darkness right out of me.

"What do I do now?" I ask the wind, but it only howls in response before dying down, leaving my skin tingling with its absence. I look up at the sky. It's an ocean of gray clouds, low and flat and swollen with unfallen rain or maybe snow.

The wind comes again, this time from behind, and I let it move me forward. I slip my hands into the coat pockets to warm them. The fingers of my right hand brush against soft paper. It's a five-dollar bill. I stare at it and then down at my bare feet.

I should buy some shoes.

And then I should go to school.

Most stores are closed at this early hour, but down the block I see a bright red awning being rolled open by a guy in jeans and a T-shirt. He must be freezing. The awning says 99CENT PLUS! As I approach, the guy yanks up the metal security gates covering the front windows and door, and starts pulling things out of the entryway onto the sidewalk—two white buckets of fake flowers, a torn cardboard box filled with black vinyl belts, a stack of white plastic lawn chairs.

I'm not sure he's officially open yet, so I just walk right by him inside before he can stop me.

"Do you have shoes?" I ask, turning as I hear him walk in behind me. "I need some shoes. And maybe a hat." He just stares at me. "It's real cold outside."

"Slippers are by the dog food," he finally answers, going behind the counter so he can watch me in the security monitor. "End of the first aisle."

I follow his directions, my feet breaking out in pin-pricks of pain as they warm up. "Just slippers? What about shoes?"

"No shoes. Just slippers. By the dog food," he answers. "Hats are there too."

At the end of the first aisle I find a plastic bin overflowing with pairs of pastel slippers made out of cheap terry cloth. They are the kind with just a strip of fabric that goes over your foot, leaving your heel and toes exposed. They'll do until I get to school and put on my gym shoes. I pick out a blue pair in my size and then study the knit hats that are hanging above the slippers. There are eight of them, and they are all bright orange.

I bring the slippers and a hat up to the counter. The man studies me for a moment, taking in my chopped-off hair, the makeup, the MTA coat, the dress, my disgusting bare feet, and I know in a second he's going to pick up the phone and call the cops. He surprises me, though, and asks. "You want socks?"

I sigh gratefully. "Mister, that's the best idea I've heard all day."

"What color?" he asks, gesturing to the hanging strip of socks behind him. I'm not sure why socks warrant the extra security of being kept behind the counter, but I'm not about to ask.

This time, I can feel the darkness coming. I grab on to the counter as my vision narrows to pinpricks, and then to nothing. My brain takes a second to catch up when I come to. The man behind the counter is saying something. He looks annoyed. "Color?" he asks again.

"Um . . ." I look down at the blue slippers. "Purple, I guess?"

He nods and pulls down the socks, handing them to me. Thankfully, they're knee-highs, but unthankfully, they are decorated with hearts and bunnies that are missewn, so both look like they're bleeding.

"Wow, they feel so good," I moan happily once I've pulled them on. They're thin, cheap polyester for sure, but they're warmer than nothing. And once I have the ugly slippers on over them, the feeling starts to come again to my toes.

I buy a giant bottle of water from the fridge by the counter and drain it all before I've even left the store. When I lower the bottle, I see the man watching me with wide eyes.

"Thirsty," I tell him, handing him the empty bottle. "Could you please trash this for me?"

He nods, takes the bottle, and watches me leave.

REMEMBERING

CHAPTER 4

R ehab was all right. I guess.

My doctor was Dr. Friedman. We met every day. She smelled like campfire.

Technically the Center for New Beginnings wasn't even really rehab, though I would never tell Seemy that. She'd never let me forget it if she found out I went to *rehab lite*, or that I kind of liked it. What kind of loser *likes* fake rehab? The thing is, once I stopped feeling like my guts had been pulled out through my nose, the feeling I had most when I first got there was relief. There was no one to perform for at New Beginnings. There wasn't anybody I had to be other than myself. And it wasn't like I had to go through some trite *I don't even know who I am!* type thing. I knew who I was. I just didn't know who I was without Seemy. I had six weeks to find out.

"Seemy says I'm just having a little Nanapocalypse."

Dr. Friedman raised her eyebrows but didn't say anything, which meant she wanted me to keep talking. Instead I stared at her eyebrows. They were furry and wild and almost met in the middle of her face, and I'd gotten really attached to them in my three days at New Beginnings. I wanted to know if they were long enough to braid, and I admired her for keeping them wild. Most people couldn't pull a look like that off without looking unkempt, but Dr. Friedman had an amazing superhero-size chin that balanced her eyebrows perfectly. She favored oversize, deconstructed sweaters and skirts in muted purples and olive green, and tasseled scarves as big as tablecloths wrapped around and around her neck, making a little nest for her giant chin.

We sat in her office, which she'd outfitted with lots of tapestry throw pillows in earth tones. And ferns. Lots of ferns. There was a burnt-orange rug with fibers so long it bordered on shag. The wooden shelves were lined with clothbound books and exotic-looking knickknacks. She kept the overhead light off, used lamps with heavy shades instead. The place was so pointedly warm and inviting it put me to sleep the first time I came in. Then again, I think I may still have been drunk.

I got tired of staring at her eyebrows and shifted in my chair, the movement pulling at the stitches in my forehead. I winced, ran my fingers lightly over them, trying to count the raised ridges of surgical thread.

"Do your stitches hurt?" Dr. Friedman finally asked.

I smirked at her. "Would you give me something if they did?"

"I can ask the shift supervisor to give you Tylenol."

"With codeine?" I asked, with fake hope.

"What do you think?"

I shrugged, ran my fingers over the stitches again. "I thought they'd be bigger."

The eyebrows went back up, and she waited for me to continue.

"They said I had fourteen stitches. I thought it'd look more impressive or something."

"Impressive to whom?"

I cleared my throat to keep from groaning aloud. "Me. Nobody. Everybody. I don't know."

"What about Seemy, your friend you just mentioned? Would you want them to impress her?"

"Best friend," I corrected her, even though I wasn't sure it was true anymore. She waited for me to continue. I won-

dered if she ever counted up the minutes she spent waiting for people to keep talking. I wondered if she could fall
asleep with her eyes open. "And I don't know . . . I guess."

"You guess what?"

"I guess it'd be cool if my stitches impressed her." I
squirmed a little in my chair, uncomfortable with the
honesty.

"Why is that?"

"Because maybe then she'd believe I need to be here."

"She doesn't believe you need help?"

I shook my head.

"Why not?"

"Because I don't drink as much as she does. She thinks
I'm a fake."

"A fake what?"

Her question caught me off guard, and I laughed
uncomfortably. "That's a really good question. Um . . . a
fake drunk? A fake friend? I don't know. . . ." I trailed off,
and we sat there in silence for a long time. "She wants me
to be dangerous. Wants *us* to be dangerous," I finally said.

"Dangerous how?"

"The way we dress, the way we act, the way we drink.
Everything. But it's never enough. I'm never dangerous
enough to keep her."

"To keep her what?"

I looked at Dr. Friedman. "Just to keep her. Interested. Happy. I don't know."

"And this is the friend who gave your overdose a nickname?"

I shifted in my seat. "It sounds stupid when *you* say it."

"And how does it sound when you say it?"

"Funny."

Dr. Friedman nodded. "And sitting here, with me, do you find this funny?"

Part of me wanted to laugh, just because she looked so serious when she asked the question. But I told the truth instead. "It's not funny at all."

"Well," she said, smiling so wide her eyebrows stretched out. "That's a start."

TODAY

I don't want to go back toward the subway. The cops might be looking for me. So I take the long way to school. I know I need to ditch MTA guy's jacket as soon as I can, but I can't bear to part with it.

I sing to keep warm, using the rhythm of my slippers slap-slap-slapping on the sidewalk.

I used to go to high school across town, on First Avenue. It was fine, I guess. I had friends there, but not many, and we weren't that close. I used to count them, my friends, and it always felt like a light handful, a number with enough room to shake around in your palm. Seemy, though, she filled my hands, both of them. And I didn't need anybody else.

Mom didn't know I was skipping school last year until after the Nanapocalypse. She called the school to tell them I was going to rehab and would be out, and they told her I couldn't come back even if I made up the work because I'd missed too many days already. It wasn't even that many days. Five, tops. Two in the fall, and three in the spring, after we'd found the carriage house.

Tick goes to kindergarten next door to my old school now, which I feel bad about because Mom was so excited when he got assigned to that school because it meant I could take him every day. So Mom has to rush there in the morning for drop-off and pay someone else to bring him back home at the end of the day.

But not today, not this week. He's staying with Dad while Mom's away, so he's bringing Tick into the city every morning and picking him up in the afternoon. Dad asked if I wanted to stay with him too, but I said no.

Mom was on the phone all summer, getting me into a new high school on Eighteenth Street. It's not as good of a school as my old one, but we were lucky to find a place close to home that would take me. There is a set of black double doors at the top of the school's front steps. And when I turn the corner, I see they're already closed. That means I'll have to ring the buzzer and get the security guard to let me in. That means I may have missed homeroom, maybe even first period, and that means they'll report me to my mom, and that means everything is going to split open again.

I scuff up the stairs as fast as my slippers will allow and jam my finger on the buzzer. There's no response.

"Oh, come *on!*" I groan aloud, buzzing again.

Finally a youngish guy in a blue security guard uniform and hat opens the door but blocks me as I try to hurry through. "ID?" he asks.

Realization floods me with panic.

"Where's my bag?" I ask him and myself at the same time. He snorts at me. I spin in a circle, like maybe I've been wearing my backpack the whole time and just didn't notice. "Please. Please, this can't be happening." My voice is shaking, and I feel like I'm going to scream myself to pieces right here on the front steps.

My backpack has everything in it. My cell phone, my wallet, my school ID, my textbooks. If I lost my backpack, I can't just walk into school right now, change my clothes, and pretend like this morning never happened. Even if I try to replace everything, my mom will find out. I know she will. And everything will unravel. That stupid backpack is the only thing standing between me moving on with my life and everything going to shit.

"No," I say. My voice is too loud. "It's fine. Everything's going to be fine. I'll go inside and get a day pass at the front office. Then I'll go home at lunch and get my ID, because I'm sure that's where my backpack is. Right? Right."

The security guard smirks. "ID?" he says again.

"I'm late, man, can you please just let me in?" I ask, standing awkwardly with one foot on the front step and one foot inside the door.

I can feel a patch of darkness coming, like a blanket being pulled over my scalp and over my eyes. I shake my head, hard, but it does nothing. I come to and it's only been a moment, because the guard is saying, "Don't call me 'man'. You need an ID to come inside." He looks down at my feet. "And shoes."

"Sorry, *lady*," I answer, "but my ID is at home and I *am* wearing shoes."

He snorts in reply. "You can't come in without an ID."

I can see over his shoulder into the front hall; the clock says 7:42, and that means I have exactly twenty-three minutes, until 8:05 a.m., to get to the front office without being marked late before first period starts.

"Don't lie, you know I can get a day pass."

"You can't come in without—"

"Seriously"—my voice gets all whispery and high-pitched like it does right before I'm going to cry—"I'm having a really, really crummy morning, and if I don't get into school before the next bell rings, I'm going to catch all kinds of hellfire."

He's not impressed, doesn't move aside.

"Weren't you ever a kid?" I ask.

He snorts. "Once. A lifetime and five minutes ago."

"Good," I say. "Then you remember how shit like being late for school can snowball. I'm just trying not to get buried, you know?" He keeps watching me, and something changes in his face, softens a little. "I'm freezing out here, man," I whisper. "I just want to come in and go to school. How can you punish a kid for wanting to go to school?"

"Fine," he says, moving aside, and I push past him into the warmth of the building. "Find your ID!" he calls after me.

REMEMBERING

The day I met Seemy was a Saturday. The first Saturday after school let out for the summer. The first Saturday of being in the netherworld between sophomore and junior year.

I woke up with Tick's butt in my face. He was sleeping on his side in just his underwear, bent like a paper clip, knees curled up so his feet pressed into my belly, the rest of him doubled over, hugging my pillow.

"My hair conditioner stopped working last night," Tick informed me, yawning and rolling over to face me. "So I came and slept with you." He shivered a little. "Now I'm cold."

I picked some sleep out of the corner of his eye and flicked it across the room and then pulled the blanket up over him, leaned up to switch the AC to low. "Why didn't you go sleep with Mom?"

"She was working," he said, "and I wanted to sleep."

I stretched. "Well, at least she's working."

Tick nodded and then asked, "Is it still summer?"

I snorted. "School just ended three days ago."

He blinked at me for a second and then said, "Oh."

Tick's kind of a melancholy kid. Maybe not melancholy, just serious. He's a thinker, my mom says. And now I was watching him wrinkle up his little brow and think so hard about summer vacation that he started to drool a little bit. I let him think, and let my own mind wander. Our home is a quiet home. Once I read a profile of this comedian and she said, "Growing up, our house was filled with laughter." I read that and thought, *Our house is full of thinking.* Back when we all spent time at Dad's, before Mom started making excuses for having to get back to the city whenever we visited, Dad would tease Mom and Tick and me. He would say, "I have been sitting here watching you all not talk to each other for the past five minutes. You're sitting right next to one another! Are you communicating telepathically?" Tick would smile shyly, jump onto Dad so he could burrow into him, and say, "Dad, we're just thinking!"

Dad would always ask what we were thinking about, which struck us as a weird question. We never asked one another that. If we thought of something important, we'd say it.

I cuddled up next to Tick and thought about how summer was here, and I was still me and that it kind of broke my heart. I wanted to shake myself off, like a dog coming out of water. Sometimes the urge to scream was so strong I would bite at the collar of my T-shirt until the feeling passed.

It wasn't that I hated myself. I just hated how afraid I was. I towered over most people, so I slouched, which barely helped at all. I wore the most basic, boring clothes I could find, to avoid standing out even more. I'd inherited my mom's voice, with its volume and texture that turned heads from across the room. The fact was that I lived in fear of people looking at me, and at the same time all I wanted to do was stand out.

Tick sighed. "Last night I dreamed it was winter and we were putting the plastic stuff on the windows to keep out the wind, except it wasn't plastic, it was cereal."

"That was just a dream. It's still summer for a long time yet."

"Oh. Okay."

From the other end of the apartment there was the click and squeak of Mom's bedroom door opening. "There's

Mom," Tick said, smiling. Neither of us moved. We stayed there, looking at each other and listening to the floors creak as she made her way through our apartment. The Tick is six years old and didn't get the sort of burly physicality that strikes the women in our family. He looks like his dad. Slight, wiry, a smile that seems almost too big for his face. He has our hair, though. Unruly and puffy and sticking out in all directions. Mom did this awesome drawing of the three of us for our Christmas card last year. It's just our silhouettes, but with our crazy hair you can totally tell it's us. She called the picture our family crest. The only bummer was that it made the Tick cry because Dad wasn't in it.

We listened to Mom make her way through our apartment. It took a while because our apartment's huge, but not because we're super rich. We're on the top floor of an old brick building in SoHo that used to be filled with garment shops. Mom and her friends moved in right after college, but she was the only one who would sign the lease. Everyone else moved out eventually, but Mom stayed on, and since the place is rent-controlled, she says the only way she's leaving is feetfirst. When she and her friends first moved in, the place was a huge, raw, open space. There was a pile of half-finished bras that reached the ceiling in the middle of the floor. They built walls to form art studios and bedrooms, put in a bathroom and a kitchen.

They did everything themselves, even some of the electrical, which is why when you flush the toilet, the light in the kitchen flickers. When everyone else moved out, Mom tore down some of the walls to make a large art studio, three bedrooms, and a giant living room.

The floors slant and it's drafty in winter and the grout in our bathroom is falling out in chunks and most of our furniture is stuff from flea markets upstate, but Mom says it doesn't matter as long as it's clean and filled with love. Barf.

The building owners have been trying for years to get us to move out, but Mom's got a really good lawyer and says we're here to stay. They renovated the whole building around us. On all of the floors below us are condos, sleek and clean with metal and glass and "architectural" bathroom fixtures, which means square sinks. On our floor, the top floor, they won't even replace the lightbulbs in the moldy-smelling hallway outside the elevators. We do that ourselves.

"There you are," Mom said as she opened my bedroom door. "Did you two keep cool last night?"

She walked over and sat on the foot of my bed, and Tick immediately crawled into her lap. She was dressed already, which meant she'd worked all night without sleeping and then showered and dressed to wake herself up.

"What are you making, Mom?" Tick asked.

Mom groaned. "It's either a big fat mess or a mixed-media installation about mall culture and female genital mutilation."

"Oh."

Mom looked at me and smiled. "You sleep okay?"

I closed my eyes and burrowed under my pillow. "I still want to sleep more. It's summer."

"But it's farmer's market day!" she said, reaching out to pull my long hair from under the pillow so she could play with it. I loved it when Mom played with my hair, but this morning I wished I could just hack it off. "It's going to be hot today. We can go to the market early, then maybe go to the pool with the Tick's dad out in Brooklyn."

I sat up and watched her closely as I asked, "Can we stay over at Dad's? Go out to brunch all together tomorrow morning?"

Tick looked at her, his face full of hope.

Her smile was a little forced. "Sure. Sounds like fun."

"Yeah!" Tick scrambled off the bed. "I'm going to pack!"

Mom and I both knew she was lying. Spending the night at Dad's didn't sound like fun for her, it sounded like murder, and she'd probably end up bailing as soon as we met up with Dad and she'd leave us in Greenpoint and tell me to bring the Tick home tomorrow. But I let myself believe for a second that things were just like they used to be. They used to love each other, I told myself, and sometimes love comes back.

"I should really get some friends," I told her, rolling over. "I can't spend the whole summer with my mom and little brother at the pool. It's bad for my reputation."

I really had only a few friends from school, and they all were taking off for the summer. Eight weeks as camp counselors, or bicycling through Europe, or at their country houses. I think Mom was glad they were all gone. The fact that they were in a different tax bracket made her prickly.

"You have friends," she assured me, "but they're the sort that bail on the city in the summer, so . . ." She trailed off.

To my mom, bailing on New York City in the summer is a sign of weakness and untrustworthiness in a person. It's the sign of someone who will steal your dog and tell lies about you. "You don't abandon your girl when she's down," Mom says, making staying in the hot, gross, stinky city overrun with tourists for the summer a badge of loyalty.

Mom went to help Tick get ready, so I brushed my teeth and washed my face and started kicking at the clothes on my bedroom floor, looking for something that seemed at least a little clean.

"I hate all my clothes," I called to Mom, finally picking up a pair of jean cutoff shorts and a tank top.

"So, do some babysitting and I'll give you money to get new clothes," Mom called back. I could hear her trying to get the Tick to brush his teeth.

"They'd just suck too," I mumbled, slumping onto my bed and dropping the shorts and top back on the floor. I knew I'd just go to the same stores, buy the same sort of things I had at home already, except maybe a different size because I'd gotten taller. Again. There was no way I could get away from my own lameness. I was hopeless and itchy and I wanted to shake out of my own skin. I'd be stuck with myself all summer, and then when school came, maybe I'd make a halfhearted effort to get a new look, but then I'd go broke or lose interest or get scared and end up looking just like myself. Boring. And giant. There were no makeovers that didn't involve sawing off a few inches of height and girth that could turn me from an ogre into an imp.

"Nan, let's go!" Mom called from the kitchen. I could hear the Tick digging out our stash of canvas shopping bags from under the sink. I was looking in my closet when I caught a glint of light reflected from the back. It was the space reserved for stupid things my mother made me wear. I reached back and yanked a truly horrendous red checked Christmas dress with shiny brass buttons off its hanger and held it up to the light. She'd bought it for me last year, when we were invited to the dean of her college's house for a holiday party. I don't know what she was thinking. It was a little-kid dress, even if it came in my gigantic size. I wore it because she paid me $10, but I looked ridiculous, like a grown-up dressed like a little girl for Halloween. What I'd forgotten, though, was that the dress had this built-in black slip with a puffy crinoline skirt, and standing there in front of my closet, I had one of those lightning-bolt ideas that you know might change your life.

"What are you wearing?" Mom laughed when I came out of my room. I spun around, fluffing the black slip's skirt as I did, ending in a pose that was half superhero, half supermodel.

"I'm wearing the most awesome dress ever," I answered matter-of-factly. I'd paired it with a pair of black yoga pants, which I planned to replace with fishnet tights as soon as I could.

"It's awfully . . ." Mom faltered, searching for the right word.

"'Awfully awesome' is the phrase you're looking for." I spun around again, and the Tick started running around me in a circle, trying to hide under my skirt.

My mom told me I wasn't going out of the house until I put on real clothes.

"These *are* real clothes."

"You can see your boobs."

"I'll put on a bra."

"It will show."

"Well, then everyone will know I'm wearing one."

"You know we're going straight from the farmer's market to Tick's dad's, so you'll be on the subway in that."

My heart leaped. "I hadn't thought of that!"

"But why?" she asked. "Why do you want to wear *that*?"

I proudly gave her the only answer I knew she couldn't argue with. "It's my ART."

The farmer's market in Union Square happens a bunch of times a week, but we always go on Saturdays. Farmers from the Hudson Valley come down and fill the west side of the park with tables, selling their goods. It's a crowded mix of veggies dumped into plastic bins and fancy jelly that costs $12 a jar. We always go early, because by midmorning the place is totally clogged with everyone from gourmet chefs to tourists to regular people like us. For some reason that Saturday it got crowded early, and there was no room for the Tick to ride his skateboard without hitting people, so Mom bought us a pint of blueberries and asked me to take him over to the wide steps that line the south side of the park.

I watched him try to ollie, then I spit blueberries in his general direction, making him cackle like a junior madman, "You missed me!"

I heard someone else laugh and looked over, and sitting on the steps a few yards away was a girl about my age. Her hair was short, the sort of little pixie cut my big old pumpkin face could never take, and she was wearing this sort of hippie, flowy embroidered dress.

"Is he your little brother?" she asked, moving closer and sitting down next to me.

"Yep." I stole another glance at her. She had a pointy chin, a spray of freckles across her nose and cheeks. I thought she smelled like strawberries. "That's the Tick."

She raised her eyebrows.

"He breast-fed till he was, like, four," I explained.

She pulled her knees up and rested her chin on them. "Cool dress."

I flushed. "Thanks." I knew she would never have talked to me if I were in my normal boring jeans and T-shirt. "Yours too."

"Not really." She groaned with a smile. "I wish my parents would let me dress like you."

I nodded in understanding. "Parents suck. My mom made me get up at eight."

The girl laughed again. "I was up at four."

My jaw dropped, and I held out the blueberries. "You win."

She laughed again, and she had this great throaty laugh

that seemed deeper than it should for someone her size. "I'm Seemy," she said. "Well, really Samantha, but everybody calls me Seemy."

She held out her hand and I shook it. "I'm Nan."

"Do you live around here?"

"SoHo. You live upstate?"

She broke into a huge smile. "Actually," she said excitedly, "we're moving back to the city. My parents have an apartment down here, on Avenue B, but they freaked out after 9/11 and bought a farm. The *Times* wrote an article about them." She shrugged. "But now they're going crazy because of all the small-town politics. We're actually moving back this summer. I'm so excited. I couldn't take Hicktown anymore."

"Cool."

We sat there, eating blueberries, watching the Tick, until she looked at her cell phone and said she had to go check in with her parents.

"We're moving down next week. Here." She handed me her phone. "Give me your number, I'll call you when I get in."

And that was the beginning of everything. It was even the beginning of the end. We just didn't know it yet.

TODAY

wish I had time to shower in the gym. I want to let hot water run all over me. I want to spread out my fingers and hold my palms up and feel the water pelt my skin. I feel like I could tip my head to the side, let the water stream into one ear and out the other, cleaning out my brain, and then I could think new thoughts.

But there's no time for that.

I need to wash up quickly and check in at the main office so I don't get marked absent.

I pull the plastic shopping bag of gym clothes from my locker and bring it with me to the girls' bathroom.

I should call Mom. But if I call Mom, things are

going to break open and spill out and she might not like what she sees when she studies the entrails. She's going to want me to answer the question that I don't even want to ask.

What happened to me last night?

I take off the MTA jacket, hang it up on the hook on the back of the stall door, and start digging through the shopping bag. I first put on the black yoga pants I wear for gym, and then reach back in to get my T-shirt and sports bra, but neither is there.

"Oh man," I groan, remembering I brought them home last week to wash. I'll have to stick with the pink dress. At least I have a pair of sneakers. I put them on, gather the shopping bag and the jacket over my arm, and walk out to the row of sinks and mirrors.

And then I drop everything onto the floor and lurch toward the mirror because I see now there is something scrawled in black marker across my chest.

HELP ME

The letters are uneven and messy, sloping down at the end, like they were scribbled in a hurry. I run my fingers over the words, and the skin feels bruised, like whoever wrote them was trying to carve them into my skin.

HELP ME

The tile floor starts to tip and sway, and I grip the edge of the sink and squat down, resting my forehead against the cool porcelain until the world steadies itself again. "Why is this happening to me?" I whisper, staring at the pipe that curves under the sink and into the wall. "Why is this happening?"

I don't want to stand back up; I don't want time to start again. I want to stay here, under the sink, until my own inertia seeps into the rest of the universe and nothing ever moves forward again.

But then my thighs are starting to cramp and my fingers are starting to hurt from holding on so tightly to the sink, and so I pull myself back up and there I am again, in the mirror.

A second later I'm tearing off a sheet of paper towel, soaking it in the sink, and wiping it across my chest. The letters stay. I wipe again, harder this time, but all that happens is the skin around the letters gets red and raw.

HELP ME, the words say. "I'm trying!" I hiss, pumping soap from the dispenser onto my hands and soaping up my chest, wiping again, groaning when I see it's not coming off. The fact is I wrote on myself. Even if I don't remember it, I can guess why I did it. I can guess that last night, alone for the first time in months in our empty apartment, I freaked out and cut open the futon in my room, which Seemy and I covered in duct tape last summer. Before we covered it, we stuck a fifth of whiskey in the cushion "for emergencies." I could say I forgot about it after the Nanapocalypse, but that'd be a lie. I knew it was there, and even if I never planned on drinking it, I liked having at least one secret from Mom left. Last night I cut the futon open, pulled out the bottle, drank myself sick, and then went out on the town. Found a costume. Some face paint. And then when I stumbled home, I bet I went into the bathroom and screamed at myself in the mirror for being so pathetically weak and then scrawled these words across my chest before drinking some more and going back out.

"Congratulations," I say to myself in the mirror. "You've ruined everything."

Dr. Friedman said sometimes when you find yourself in a mess, you have to clean up what you can and leave the rest as a lesson learned.

I pry open the paper towel dispenser so I can take out the whole roll, then climb up onto the left-hand sink, stick my feet into the sink on the right, and set my sneakers on the shelf below the mirror. I pull the yoga-pant legs as high up as they can go, and crank as much soap as I can out of the dispenser and go to work washing the filth off my legs and feet. I get the water as hot as I can stand it; block the drain with my heel so the sink fills up. I let the water drain just before it reaches the rim, and start to scrub. The water swirls black in the sink. I scrub and scrub and scrub, scrub it all away until the skin on my feet and legs is pink and tingling.

I try to give my face the same scrubbing treatment, but it doesn't work as well. Some of the white comes off, but it leaves a sort of glowing shadow on my skin, and the black stays stuck to my lips and eyes. There was a time I would have been flat-out thrilled to look like this, but I never had the guts to push it this far. Seemy used to roll her eyes at me, leaning in to block my view of myself in the mirror in the bathroom at Duke's or wherever we'd gone to put my makeup on. "Just leave it," she'd say as I wiped at my face with toilet paper, "it looks good. Fierce. You'll ruin it!" Sometimes she'd call me a coward. She'd say, "I thought you were this badass, but you're totally not. You're, like, the least scary person I know." And she'd say this to me while wearing glitter on her cheeks and a kid's superhero cape. To her I became like an uncooperative Barbie doll.

I wish she would get out of my head.

I hold out my arm and rinse off the four cuts and flinch at the pain as the water runs over them. I can't stop staring at the way they curve from my inner elbow to my wrist. Four rivers on a map to my memories. I pat them dry with a paper towel and put on the MTA jacket, covering them up.

REMEMBERING

Tick and I shared the sill of one of the oversize windows in the den, watching the street below for Seemy and her parents. The windows are big enough for us to stand in, starting just a foot from the floor and ending ten feet up, almost to the ceiling. Mom hates it when we stand in them, because the windows rattle in their casements when it is windy. She worries that one day the windows will come loose and plummet to the sidewalk below while we cling to them with white knuckles, our eyes closed against the glass so we won't see what's coming. It was 9 p.m., past Tick's bedtime, but Mom said he could stay up until Seemy got here.

"It's finally getting dark," Tick said, leaning his head against the glass and looking down at the sidewalk below. "I hate going to bed when it's not dark."

"Me too."

"Is that them?" He pushed a finger against the glass, and down on the street I saw Seemy walking with two people I had to guess were her parents. They were looking at the building numbers as they walked, and I was suddenly embarrassed to be watching for them. I stepped quickly off the ledge and flopped onto the couch.

As soon as I did, the intercom let out its dying *landlord-won't-fix-me* buzz. Tick jumped off the window ledge and ran to our front door.

"I get to open it when they come up!" he announced, already holding the doorknob. "Come on, Nan! Get the intercom!"

My mom came out of her studio, wiping her hands on the hem of her smock. "Is that them?"

"Yes," I groaned, getting off the couch and walking over to the door. I paused with my hand on the intercom phone. "Can everyone please just relax and not embarrass me?"

My mom crossed her eyes, stuck out her tongue, and then said, "You're the one wearing a Halloween costume."

I realized I was wearing the same slip dress as the day I met Seemy, and suddenly I wished I were wearing something else. She'd seen me in this already, but there was no time to change.

I picked up the intercom phone and held it away from my ear so it could crackle and pop and snap without making me go deaf. "What's up, Chuck?" I spoke loudly so he could hear.

"The Turbin family is here!"

"Thanks, go ahead and send them up!"

Ten minutes later we were all sitting in the den, Seemy and I sharing the oversize armchair with the seat cushion so worn it could swallow you whole. I kept sneaking glances at her, since I hadn't seen her since the first time we met at the farmer's market. We'd talked on the phone once, when she called to tell me she was moving down this weekend, and then here she was. In our apartment. For real. It felt like my summer and the new me were both finally starting. Our moms were sitting across from each other on couches. Seemy's mom perched on the edge of our worn plaid couch, and my mom lounged back in the mismatched leather one. Seemy's dad stood, and Tick was curled up under the coffee table, asleep. It had gotten dark out, and I was glad my mom insisted on turning on only two of the lamps. It made the room cozy, and it kept some of the threadbare spots on the furniture from showing.

"We so appreciate you taking Samantha in for the night," Seemy's mom finally said. She was fine boned, like Seemy, but taller, with long, shiny black hair, flowing clothes, and the sort of artsy jewelry they sell in the glass cases in the gift shop at the Met. "We didn't anticipate the move taking so long today, and her bedroom isn't set up at all."

My mom remained reclining back, like she was the queen of Sheba. People with money always make her a bit crabby. "It's no problem," she answered with a slow smile, "we're happy to have her."

"Yeah, thanks for having me." Seemy giggled, and then she slipped off her shoes and stuck her feet under my thighs. "I'm freezing!" She giggled again, threading her arm through mine and snuggling close to me.

Seemy's dad was slowly studying the paintings that crowded against the brick walls around the den. "Are these all yours?" he asked, and I noticed Seemy's upper lip wrinkle a little at his almost accusatory tone.

Mom raised her eyebrows, took a moment to turn in her seat to face him, and then answered. "Yes."

He took another sip of lemonade and then slurped some ice. "They're pretty good." And he didn't say it like he meant it. He said it like he knew something about art, like he was some sort of painting professional and was doing her a favor by giving her a fake compliment with his mouth full of ice. For a moment we all watched my mom watch him. Her distaste was obvious.

"The Guggenheim seems to think so," she finally answered, turning back around. And I bit my tongue to keep from laughing. Mom's work is most definitely not in the Guggenheim.

Seemy's dad made a *huh* sound in his throat.

"We're big supporters of the arts," Seemy's mom said proudly. "That's one of the reasons we wanted to bring Samantha back to the city. Museums, art shows, all of the interesting artist people . . ."

"What, and sell the farm?" Mom asked, her voice dripping with sarcasm.

"We kept the farm," Seemy's dad said, finally sitting down next to her mom, and we all watched as he ran his hand over the couch cushion and then tried to hide a smirk. "The place basically runs itself."

"Well, with some help from the staff," her mom chimed in.

"You should come by our apartment in the city once we have it set up. We have quite an art collection ourselves," her father said. "Though it's a bit pared down, since we had to get Seemy into school. You know"—he looked at my mom conspiratorially—"donations."

"Speaking of, darling," her mom said, "we should go and at least get our bedroom unpacked. I'm exhausted."

"You're welcome to stay here," my mom said, standing up so suddenly it made everyone jump. "You're sitting on our guest room. Pulls out into a lovely bed."

"Oh my God," I groaned, watching our parents study each other, trying to figure out who was winning this weird competition of who could be the biggest jerk.

"Nah, we've got to run. Seemy," her dad said, "behave yourself." Then he responded to a nudge from his wife by reaching into his pocket. I thought, *Oh God, please no, please don't offer my mother money.* He pulled out a roll of bills, peeled off a few, and handed them to Seemy. "Take everyone out for breakfast tomorrow morning." He smiled at my mom. "To say thanks for their . . . hospitality."

There was a long moment in which I think we all wondered if my mom would throw Seemy's dad out the window. But she didn't.

Later on, when Mom had gone into her studio to work, and the Tick had gone to bed, I opened up the futon chair in my room for Seemy to sleep on.

"Sorry my parents were so weird," Seemy said, sitting on the floor next to my bed, flipping through the small stack of records on the shelf below the nightstand. "They get freaked out around real New Yorkers. I think they feel like frauds."

"Why? I thought they were from here." I stretched a sheet over the futon, tucking in the edges.

"Nah, they're from Florida. Panhandle. Can we play this one?" She pulled out a record, tipping it so the vinyl slipped out of the sleeve. She caught it with her fingers, leaving prints on the shiny vinyl.

I hurried over, taking the record from her, holding it carefully along the rim. "Here, let me." I felt bad for basically snatching it out of her hands. "It's my dad's." I lifted the clear plastic cover of the record player with my pinky and set the record on the turntable, switched it on, and carefully placed the needle down. "So we just have to be careful."

There was the soft, familiar, reassuring popping static sound before the music started. I picked up the record sleeve and handed it to Seemy. "It's Odetta. I love her. I wish she hadn't died, I really wanted to see her play."

Seemy studied the picture on the front of the record. "It's so cool you have records. I wish they still made them."

I laughed. "They do still make them. Lots of punk bands still put out vinyl."

"No way, really?"

"Sure." I hoped she wouldn't ask me anything else,

because aside from the fact that bands still put out vinyl, I knew nothing else about it. "Anyway. My mom's from Maine. It's New York, nobody's from here. That's the whole point."

"Where's your dad from?"

I went back to making the bed, spreading out a thin comforter and putting a fresh case on the pillow. A long moment passed, and I wasn't sure what to say.

"Sorry," Seemy said. "I didn't mean to pry."

"It's all right." I sat down on the futon. "The deal is that I don't know who my actual dad is. He was a sperm donor. The Tick's dad lives in Brooklyn, in Greenpoint. He and my mom were going to get married before the Tick was born, so I started calling him Dad. They never got married, but the name stuck, I guess."

There was a long silence, and I realized I was shaking. Telling the truth like that, just everything all at once, wasn't something I was used to.

"Wow," Seemy finally said.

"Yeah," I agreed, "Wow."

Seemy climbed up on the futon next to me. "So do you still see him, Tick's dad?"

"We go out on weekends sometimes. It's technically just the Tick's visit, but I go too. And Tick spends two weeks there in the summer."

"My ex-boyfriend used to do that," Seemy said solemnly. "Two weeks with his dad every summer, and every other weekend I wouldn't get to see him. Sucked."

"That does suck," I agreed, standing up. "Do you need anything else? An extra blanket or anything? The AC only has two settings—off and frigid."

"Nah, I'm good," Seemy said.

The next morning I woke up to find Seemy and the Tick sitting on the futon playing go fish.

TODAY

"You're late," snaps Sheila, the front-office administrator, standing up from behind her desk as soon as I push open the office door. "I saw you out the window, and I know you've been here for thirty minutes already."

"I had to go to the bathroom," I tell her, laying my arms on the high wooden counter that divides the office. The room swings sideways a little bit, and I feel my eyes flutter closed. I rest my forehead on my wrists until the feeling stops.

"Are you okay?" Sheila asks.

No. Definitely not.

"I'm fine. Just some lady troubles," I explain, taking a breath and standing up straight, keeping the fingers of one hand pressed lightly against the counter, hoping it will help me keep my balance.

"Mmm-hmmm," Sheila says, crossing her arms to glower down at me from her side of the counter. She's obviously not convinced. "Glad to see you found some proper shoes at least, though I'd rather you had found some makeup remover."

I try to wiggle my eyebrows in what I hope is an endearing way, though my voice comes out hollow and strange. "It was a Halloween costume gone horribly, horribly wrong."

Sheila raises her eyebrows at me. "Class and name?"

"Junior. Masterson," I answer.

Sheila types something, and then I see her add something next to my name. "ID, please."

"It's at home." It's too hot in here. And there's that smell, like industrial cleaner.

She glances down at the screen. "That's your third lost ID."

"It's not lost," I explain. "It's at home."

"Doesn't matter," Sheila says, and then pauses for the first-period bell to ring. "It's not here now, and this is your third strike."

I shrug, at a loss. "Sorry." She just keeps staring at me

and my stomach goes a little funny. "Is that . . . bad?"

She pulls a familiar-looking form printed on yellow paper out of the wire paper organizer on the desk. She slides it across to me. It's an ID request form. "You lose three IDs, you pay two hundred fifty dollars and get a one-day in-house suspension."

Whoa, no. There's a loud *whooshing* noise inside my head, the kind of sound your life makes when it's swirling down a toilet. "I . . . I didn't know that."

"It's in the student handbook."

I gulp and try to keep my voice calm. "There's a student handbook?" I squeak.

Sheila actually looks a little bit sorry for me, which makes me want to cry even more, because I don't deserve her pity. I did this, whatever this is, to myself. "And you signed a piece of paper when you started here saying you'd read it. All students do. Sound familiar?"

Oh God, that *does* sound familiar! I'm such an idiot. SUCH. AN. IDIOT.

"Look." I take a deep, shuddering breath, "I can't get a suspension."

"Then you should have brought in your ID. It's a one-day in-house suspension. No big—"

"No, you don't understand!" My words tumble out. "I'm sorry to be totally freaking out on you, I know you didn't write the rules and you're probably a really nice person, but seriously, I *can't* get suspended!" I can feel my heart straining, cracking, splintering. "I promised my parents I wouldn't mess up anymore."

Sheila sighs at me, hands me a tissue from the flowered box on her desk, and says, "This is what I'm going to do. I'm going to give you a day pass. Come in tomorrow, bring your ID, and we'll be good. Don't bring in your ID, and I'm filing a report and you'll get the suspension. Understood?"

"Yes. Understood. Thank you." I snivel, wiping my nose. "Thank you. I can get it tonight."

Apparently, that's too much information for Sheila, because she snaps, "Just bring it in tomorrow," pushing a clipboard with a xeroxed form across the counter. "Fill this out, it's your day pass."

I scribble in my name and student ID number, and then sign and date it.

She signs it, stamps it, and hands the form back to me. "Find your ID."

REMEMBERING

Seemy was freckles and two tiny pigtails at the nape of her neck. She was wiry arms and delicate wrists and no need for a bra. She was calling men "Hey, mister" and women "Hey, lady." She was vending-machine monster tattoos and grabbing my hand when we crossed busy streets. She caused whiplash in boys.

I was broad backed and big footed. I was still growing taller. I was not thinning out. I was the not-fat sort of fat with muscled legs that don't fit into skinny jeans, a belly that was round even after the stomach flu, and hands my mother said could build an ark. I worried that I would be too big for a firefighter to rescue me. I sounded stupid when

I giggled. I sprouted tiny boobs at ten that have stayed the same size, and I got my period at eleven, and even though my mom started in on me early about loving my body and my shape and my size, it was hard not to wish it all away.

It's dumb to still be hurt that I was always too big to be the baby when I played house with my friends on the playground as a little kid. No one could pick me up to rock me to sleep.

I could never tell my mom how badly I wanted to be a wiry girl. Her entire mission as my mom was to get me to love myself for who I was, to appreciate my strength. And it's not that I didn't appreciate it. I just wished it came in a smaller package with a narrow waist and bony ankles.

I used to think that Mom and Dad getting back together was the thing I wanted most in the world. And then I met Seemy and I knew I had never truly wanted anything before, not the way I wanted her to be my friend. It was a want and a wish and a prayer and a hope that came from the same place that makes you believe in Santa, or that monsters disappear when you hide under the covers.

Seemy would laugh at me because in the beginning I always looked so surprised when she showed up for plans we had made. Once she said, *Oh, you poor, big old bear, have you even* had *friends before?* And I told her, *Not real ones. Not like you.* And she squealed, *That's so sad!* and hugged me.

There was a little park near Seemy's house that we called Twee Park. It was tiny, a grove of trees circled by a wrought iron fence that hung heavy with thick vines. A short cobblestone path led from the latched gate through the trees and opened into a small circle, a blue bench at its edge. The trees made it shady, and the early weeks of that first summer we spent hours sitting on the bench drinking iced coffee, cracking each other up and making plans for city adventures that never happened.

That was before Seemy made two declarations. The first was that both of our looks were *utterly, unforgivably forgettable.* The second was that we should probably start drinking or else our summer wasn't going to be any fun at all. Where Seemy was from upstate, kids spent summer nights around bonfires deep in the woods, drinking beer and roasting marshmallows. She made it sound like a Ralph Lauren commercial.

We'll run around the city all summer with a buzz, looking totally amazing! It will be like a movie!

I agreed. Of course I agreed. In the beginning I would have said yes to anything Seemy suggested, because for some reason she had chosen me to be her friend and the least I could do was say yes. Yes to Kahlúa in our iced coffee, and yes to erasing ourselves and starting over.

It did hurt a tiny bit because I was already making

myself over and I loved the results because they made me look like Seemy. She said, *We have to have a serious talk. Promise you won't get mad?* And then she told me I needed my own style, and then I realized I looked like her in the same way a "magic growing dinosaur" toy looks like its larger self before you drop it in water and it grows five hundred times its size. It stops being cute and starts being weird and bulbous and gross.

Seemy said I should go the other way. Away from cute. So I did what she said and I ricocheted.

Seemy puts tiny star stickers on each of her fingernails? I paint mine black with a Sharpie. Seemy buys a pair of Lolita-style oversize sunglasses in the shape of hearts? I pierce my eyebrow. And then my lip. And then my tongue.

I made myself delight in my manufactured edginess. Black clothes, black hair with rainbow stripes, platform combat boots that hiked me even taller, skull rings. It made me angry sometimes, that I was stuck being the shadow to her light. I made a T-shirt with a quote from that old band Rage Against the Machine. I tore off pieces of duct tape to make the words, and I never washed the shirt so they wouldn't come off. ANGER IS A GIFT, the shirt said. Seemy thought it was awesome, and sometimes I wore it and felt a secret prickling of pride because she didn't even know it was directed at her.

Cute little Seemy, and big bad me, tipsy masters of New York City.

But toward the end of our friendship, right before the Nanapocalypse, she started to get all prickly about the cute thing. Toad would say something to her, call her pixie or laugh when she said something serious, and she would lose her shit. Start screaming at him. Swearing. Which would make him laugh more. And it *was* kind of funny, because here was this tiny thing wearing a pair of bright red rain galoshes and a 1950s party dress roaring out streams of obscenities, and halfway through it's like she would just give up, and she would keep swearing but her voice would get higher or she would curtsy or giggle or do something that dulled her edge down to nothing and then she would sigh and say, "Nobody takes me seriously," and Toad would say, "Sure we do, pixie," and then he'd pass her the bottle.

Once, around this time, Seemy and I were walking and she stopped in the middle of the sidewalk and asked me, "Do you think I'm sexy?"

Some woman brushed by and snapped, "Very sexy, now get out of the way."

We were in SoHo, on the way back to my apartment. It was a Saturday in spring, so the sidewalk was totally clogged, and all I wanted was to get off Broadway and onto one of the side streets.

"Well?" Seemy asked. People streamed around us. Tourists looked as us, anxious for any kind of in-the-wild New Yorker moment. "Am I?" Seemy turned in a circle. Not a cutesy turn, but a matter-of-fact *Please be honest* turn. She was wearing a pair of high-waisted blue wool sailor's trousers we'd found at Beacon's Closet, a snug plain white T-shirt. It was a less adorable look than she usually went for, especially since she'd taken scissors and slit the T-shirt right down the front so the electric blue lace bra she'd stolen the other day showed through.

"You're the sexiest thing on two legs," I told her.

She scowled and stomped past me, groaning. "You just say that because you love me. Toad said the same thing."

Sometimes, near the end, when I'd go to meet her in the park before going out, I'd find her talking to the guys we called randoms who hung out there sometimes. I'd see her through the gate, sitting on the back of the bench, holding court over a group of guys who made my stomach lurch in nervous anticipation.

If you took apart the way these guys looked, dissected them with one of those online dress-your-character games, they wouldn't seem so alarming. Tattoos. So what? Preschool teachers have tattoos. And their clothes were nothing to scream in terror about either. Maybe a little worn, but nothing alarming. Jeans. T-shirts. Maybe a hooded sweatshirt or a baseball cap. Boring, right? But then you add in the scabs. Maybe one the size of a quarter on an elbow, a nick under an eye. Maybe they don't have all their teeth. Maybe their tattoos don't look like they came from an actual tattoo shop, maybe they look like they were done with a pen and razor. Maybe they have hoarse voices, maybe they move too suddenly, laugh too loud, maybe they have sunken faces and beady eyes. Maybe they punch each other sometimes and you can't tell if they're joking. Maybe they dress younger than they are. Maybe they aren't teenagers. Or even in their twenties. Maybe they're even older. Maybe they're men. Full-grown men and they're standing in a park talking to a sixteen-year-old girl, watching her like they are starving and she is the first food they've seen in days.

TODAY

After I leave Sheila in the office, I don't go to class. I need to start covering my tracks with my mom. I squeeze myself into the ancient wooden phone booth in the basement by the woodshop and call her with two quarters I find in the bottom of my shopping bag.

She doesn't pick up, so I leave her a message. "Hi, Mom, it's me. I've been having weird cell phone reception issues, and it's not letting me pick up my voice mail, so I don't know if you called. I'm on a pay phone at school, just calling to say hi and everything's fine. Hope you're having fun. Love you!"

I don't realize the darkness came until it goes away, and

I find myself holding the phone in my hand, listening to the rapid beep of a disconnected line.

I hang up the phone. I refuse to think about what's happening to my body. If I don't think about it, it's not real. It will go away. I will find my backpack and everything will go back to the way it was.

I sneak out the back door.

By the time I get to our apartment building in SoHo, I'm totally soaked. The good thing is that when it rains, our neighborhood gets a break from the tourists. They duck inside the supersize flagship stores on Broadway that are really just elephantine versions of the same stores they have in the mall back home. And then as soon as it stops raining they pour back out onto the streets in disposable transparent rain parkas printed with I LOVE NEW YORK on the back, unfolding their laminated street maps in the middle of the sidewalk in giddy clumps, totally oblivious to the actual New Yorkers who are trying to walk by.

Mom says in the old days she never used to have worry about that "element." She says it like she's talking about murderers and thieves instead of tourists. I'm not sure which she thinks is worse.

There's a film crew blocking the sidewalk in front of our apartment. I actually don't mind having to walk into the narrow street to get around them, since it drives me crazy when people make movies about New York in a place other than New York. Only assholes shoot in Vancouver and then call it New York. Only New York is New York. Our street is always in movies, since it's tree lined and the buildings are old and picturesque and it's dotted with precious little restaurants and boutiques with striped fabric awnings and faux-weathered signs hanging from curlicue iron rods that make it look charming without looking like an outdoor mall.

Our building, however, has become the eyesore of the block. It's metal and glass and looks stupid sandwiched between adorable brownstones. It wasn't always like this. It used to be old and rickety and perfect, but then the building owners renovated and threw all that charm down a yellow trash chute that emptied into a Dumpster on the sidewalk. All except for the top floor, our apartment. If you look at our building, it kind of looks like a robot wearing a brick hat.

"What's up, Chuck?" I stomp my feet on the mat just inside the front doors by the doorman's desk, pulling off my hat and shaking off the water droplets that have gathered on it.

Chuck snorts, not looking up from the tiny television he hides in the narrow space under the counter that tops his desk. He's leaning back in his chair, rotating a little from side to side, his hands resting on his belly. "Don't get water on my floor, I just mopped up."

It took me a while to get used to having a doorman, even though technically, and made repeatedly clear by the building's owners, he's not *our* doorman. He's supposed to ignore my mom and me and Tick, but Chuck's a good dude, and he always says hello and secretly signs for our packages.

"Seta turn the heat on for you yet?" I ask, blowing into my palms. "It's freezing in here."

"It's not that cold, wimp," he answers, still looking at the television.

I go to Seta's office door, to the left of the elevators, and find it locked.

"He's out," Chuck calls over.

"Shit. Lunch?"

"No, his mom's in the hospital. He won't be back until tonight. Why's your voice all crinkly?"

"Don't know. That's too bad about Seta's mom. Hope she's okay." I lean over the counter and grab a handful of the M&M's Chuck keeps next to the TV. "I need to get into our place. God, these are *good*! I'm starving." My stomach rumbles in agreement. "I left my backpack upstairs and I need to get back to school."

He finally looks up at me. "Child, what the hell happened to you?"

"What? My face? Or my hair?"

He wrinkles his nose, reeling back a little. "Your eyes. You've got crazy eyes."

"Contacts." I lie to him matter-of-factly. "Halloween costume. Supposed to make me look like one of those devil kids in the movies. So how do I get into my apartment?" I ask, my mouth still full of M&M's.

"Can't help you. Seta's gone, he has the spare keys."

"Yeah, but what if there was an emergency?"

"In the event of a true medical or safety emergency, we would have the authorities come and kick down your door. But doing that to retrieve a textbook might lessen your appeal with the building owners."

I sigh and rest my head on the counter. "I don't feel well in the stomach."

My stomach rumbles loud enough for us both to hear.

"Child, you need to eat something before you digest your own kidneys," he says. The thought of food makes my stomach go all funny. Half nauseous, half famished. I realize with a chill that I don't know the last time I ate.

"Fine, I'll go get a slice." My voice sounds hollow. "You want something?"

"Where're you going?" he asks, starting our most frequent conversation.

"Ray's."

"Forget it," he says, looking back to the TV. "I'm keeping my money."

"Who says I wasn't going to treat you?" I ask, offended.

"Because you *never* treat me," he counters, which is the truth.

"That's true. And I would have done it this time, except I can't because I won't have enough to go to Pizza Heaven and get you the ridiculous tourist pizza slices I *know* you are going to make me get."

"It's not tourist pizza," he says.

"It is because only tourists put that much crap on their pizza. Just let me go to Ray's."

"Forget it," he says, still staring at the TV. "I got my M&M's for lunch."

"You are so not from New York."

Now he actually looks at me, so sharply that I take a step back. "There are all sorts of New York, little girl," he says firmly. "You and your opinion about how to spend your doorman's money is just one of them."

"Now I feel like an asshole." I pout, looking at my sneakers. I sneak a peek and see him raising his eyebrows.

"You're not an asshole," he finally says. "You just get wrapped up in your first-world problems."

"Like how to spend my doorman's money?"

"Exactly. Now, go get me two slices, a Shoeless Joe and a Luke I Am Your Father."

I groan.

"Problem?"

I debate telling him that the only name a slice of pizza should have is regular or *maybe* pepperoni, if you're feeling frisky. But I'm starving, so I don't argue the point. "No problem. Just write down what you want, because I already forget what you said." He scribbles down his order and hands it to me, along with some cash.

I eat my pizza on one of the rainbow-painted stools at the high counter that wraps around half of Pizza Heaven. The guy at the counter glowered at me while I ordered, and for a second I wondered if Chuck was just messing with me when he wrote down the names of the slices he wanted. But he wasn't, they were right there, hanging above the pizza oven on a hand-painted menu. For myself I got a Bird, which involves buffalo wings and a ton of blue cheese, and a Dude, which is basically a pie made out of cheeseburger. They were good, I'll admit that much, but it definitely wasn't pizza.

And it definitely wasn't hot. I debated asking the glowering guy behind the counter to stick my slices back in the oven, but he kept glaring at me, so I decided against it. It's just so freaking *cold* today, and I don't think they even have the heat on in here. Cheap bastards. I want to tell them that just because it doesn't usually get cold in New York until late November, it doesn't mean that this isn't a freak year or something. It doesn't mean that it's, like, outside of the realm of freaking possibility that we might get a cold snap before Thanksgiving.

I'm so cold that to drink my Coke I have to pull the MTA guy's coat sleeve over my hand. Otherwise my fingers go numb. Before I leave, I bite the bullet and ask the grump behind the counter to stick Chuck's slices back in the oven for a few minutes.

I go into the women's bathroom while I wait, turn the water on hot, and run my hands under it until they warm up. It's hot in here, and I stuff my hat in a jacket pocket. This is what I hate about winter in New York. You're either freezing or sweating. I turn the water to cold, splash some on my face, and look at myself in the mirror. My pupils are pinpricks. I run my fingers over my shorn hair, flinch at a sore spot on my scalp.

There's just one stall in the bathroom, and I don't even notice there's someone in it until the toilet flushes.

"Hey, what's up?" An unfamiliar girl comes out of the stall. She looks like she's about my age, maybe older. She's wearing a lightweight cotton dress with a thin sweater over it. I shiver just looking at her.

"Oh, hey," I mumble, turning off the water. I feel like it looks weird to just walk out again, so I go into the stall.

"It didn't all come off, hmm?" the girl asks, raising her voice so I can hear it over the water in the sink as she washes her hands.

"Excuse me?" I ask, shaking my head because I hate having conversations with strangers while I pee.

"Your costume. The face paint," the girl answers. I hear her pull a paper towel from the dispenser.

"Have we . . . do I know you or something?"

"*Duh,*" she snorts, "I was in the bathroom at Duke's when you were trying to get it off."

I finish and flush. The girl is leaning on the sink when I come out.

"Don't you remember?" she asks, moving aside so I can wash my hands. "I gave your friend one of those Handi-Wipe things from my purse to see if it would help get the makeup off."

I close my eyes against the sudden wave of nausea that floods over me. "My friend?"

"Yeah, your friend. Skinny little thing. Wore the same dress as you."

All I can do is look at her in the mirror. A bead of sweat

drips down my forehead and slips into my eye. I blink it away.

"I was with a friend last night?"

"Yeah, at Duke's. You don't remember?"

I shake my head, and then shake it harder, trying to clear it.

She leans in a little behind me, watching my reflection in the mirror. "You all right? You don't look all right."

"Fine," I answer, before rushing by her to throw up in the toilet.

She asks once more if I'm okay, but I don't answer, and a moment later, after listening to me retch again and again, she leaves.

I black out for a while after I throw up. I don't know for how long. When I come to, I find that I've fallen and I'm slumped against the toilet. I push myself up, groaning at the soreness in my joints.

REMEMBERING

The last time I was at Duke's . . . the last time I *remember* being at Duke's was a few days after I got out of rehab. It was my first time seeing Seemy, and it was not going well.

"Seemy!" I leaned over and hissed loudly in her ear. "Sit up!"

She grinned up at me from where she lay on the cushioned vinyl seat of our booth. Then she reached under the table and peeled off a piece of gum and acted like she was about to put it in her mouth. I hit her hand, making her drop it.

"What the hell, Nan!" she whined. "I'm *hungry!*"

"Then sit up and eat your french fries." I tried to pull her into a sitting position, but she stayed limp, giggling at me as I tried. Tick had done the same thing that morning, refusing to let me get up from where we lay together on the couch, watching cartoons. He'd been sleeping with me since I got home, and I'd been dragging him around the apartment while he hung on to my leg, refusing to let me go anywhere without him. With the Tick, all I had to do was tickle him to get him to let go. With Seemy, all I wanted to do was smack her. "Fine. Just fine. Lie there if you want." I turned back to my french fries, dipped one in ketchup, and tried to swallow through the lump in my throat.

I smelled Toad before I saw him. He sat down hard next to me in the booth, taking up too much room with his teeth and his elbows and his stupid pants. "Whatsup."

"Hey, Toad." I ate another fry. He took one from my plate, and I fought the urge to punch him in the face. He jumped all of a sudden, then bent over to look under the table and cracked up. "Stop pinching, Seemy!"

He sat up and leaned back in the booth, threading his fingers together behind his head and spreading out his elbows like he was reclining on a beach. He stayed in that position for only a second before shifting again, taking another french fry, and winking at me. He was like a damn dog, pissing all over the place to claim his territory.

I wanted to tell him I got it. Duke's was his place now. His and Seemy's. And Seemy was his too.

"So, Nan," he asked, drinking my Coke, "are you having a good welcome-home-from-rehab dinner?"

Seemy cracked up and started singing that song: "They tried to make me go to rehab, I said no, no, no!"

I put down the fry I was about to eat and moved to get out of the booth, shoving Toad out of my way.

"Come on, Nan, chill out." Toad laughed, his mouth full.

Seemy suddenly regained her ability to sit up. "Don't go, Nanja!" She tried to grab my arm, spilled my Coke. I yanked my arm away, kept walking toward the door.

I passed by Edie, one of the waitresses we knew. She was leaning against the counter, watching me. "You taking them with you?" she asked.

I shook my head.

She smirked. "Please?"

As I pushed open the door, I heard her call out, "I'll give you a dollar if you do! Two if they never come back!"

TODAY

I rinse my mouth in the sink and splash water on my face, even if the makeup keeps me from feeling it. I stare at myself in the mirror and then unzip the jacket. The words across my chest read, HELP ME. And now I have this feeling, this terrible feeling that it wasn't me who was asking for help at all.

Don't ask questions you don't want the answers to, Nan. Don't ask why it feels like your body is ripping apart at the seams.

Seemy.

Leave it alone, Nan. "I can't," I say aloud.

I rush out of Pizza Heaven, Chuck's pizza box tucked under my arm.

I walk fast, my right hand pushing down so hard in the jacket pocket I can see the outline of my knuckles, like I'm trying to punch through the fabric. Why the hell are there no pay phones in New York anymore? It takes me three blocks to find one outside a bodega, next to one of those musical animal rides the Tick always begs Mom for rides on. The phone's not in a booth, it's just bolted to the side of the building.

I plug in two quarters—Chuck's change from the pizza—and dial.

A familiar, raspy voice answers. "H'lo?"

"Oh Jesus, Seemy!" I gasp with relief, tears stinging my eyes. But then she keeps talking, "Ha-ha, got you! I'm not picking up. Leave a message. Peace out."

"Sss . . ." It's like all my energy has been drained. "Seemy, it's Nan. I know . . . I know it's been a while. I think. But, can you call me? Can you call me right now?"

I don't even say good-bye, I just hang up, and then realize that she'll call my cell phone, and I don't even have my cell phone.

Cold sweat is making the plastic dress stick to my back, and I yank at the hem, trying to get it unstuck. I walk fast back toward my apartment building. There are so many cars on Broadway, and as I walk, the noises of their engines combine into a roar that threatens to crack my head open.

I duck down a side street, thankful to be away from the noise, though there is the annoying rattle of an ancient blue hatchback chugging past me down the street, its muffler vibrating with a *chug-chug-chug* sound.

I must have called her. Or she called me. However it started, we met up, and we used, and now all the promises I've made have been broken, and something is really, really wrong. I'm not sure I can bear the weight of hating myself this much again. How could I do that? How could I be so weak? She must have begged me to meet up with her. Or maybe she didn't. Maybe I begged her. Called her alone from my empty apartment, crying and pleading with her to see me. *I'm so sorry, Seemy. I'm so sorry!* Dr. Friedman lied to me. She said I was strong enough to do this. But I'm not. I'm not strong enough at all.

I walk faster.

By the time I get back to our building, I'm freezing again.

Chuck's on the phone, and I practically drop the pizza box in his lap. He takes it from me, shouldering the phone and glaring at me. I shake my hands and rub them together, trying to get the feeling back. *"It's cold!"* I whisper to him in apology.

He mouths the words *Give me my change!* I hold up my hands, showing him that they're empty, and whisper loudly, "If you wanted change, you shouldn't have sent me for tourist pizza!"

Duke's isn't far, only on Eighth Street, but I'm so cold I can't bear the thought of walking the ten blocks. And I've started to shake so much I'm not sure that I'd make it without falling over on the sidewalk, a quivering, shivering mess.

I jump the subway turnstile without paying and wait on the edge of the subway platform. At least it's slightly warmer once I'm underground. My shivering slows down to just the occasional full-body shudder. I stare down at the subway tracks, and my vision blurs a little. I back away to lean against the wall.

There's a woman in a business suit and heels standing next to me. It's one of those suits with a narrow skirt, her legs bare. She must be freezing. Out of the corner of my eye I see her pull a white folded handkerchief from her satchel and pat her forehead with it. I try not to stare, but is she *sweating*? She must be ill.

She looks at me and smiles. "It's boiling down here. You'd think they'd fix the heat so they don't fry us to death before winter even gets here."

I nod and try to smile. I look furtively around us and see dozens of moist faces, jackets taken off and slung over arms. One woman pulls at the neck of her blouse, trying to create a breeze.

I am freezing to death, and everyone else is on fire.

I pull my hat down farther, shielding my ears from the blasts of hot air that only seem to chill me.

REMEMBERING

Seemy and I always said that the discovery of the Vegetarian Dim Sum House was the official start of our best-friendship.

We'd hung out a bunch of times before, and were growing closer and closer, but it wasn't until that brutally hot summer day that things felt like they really clicked into place. We were down on Canal Street because Seemy had heard there was a place we could get matching sets of brass knuckles with our names on them. I don't know *why* she thought we could find them down there, and I warned her Canal Street was the most annoying place in the city, especially in summer, and I would rather gouge my own eyes out than go there. Canal Street is in Chinatown, but I think it gives Chinatown a bad name. Canal Street is a ten-block stretch of street filled on both sides with tiny stores selling chintsy scarves and junky jewelry and cheap electronics. But the real reason tourists flock to Canal Street like cockroaches to a bagel crumb is the illegal knockoffs. Chanel, Prada, Gucci, Fendi. Purses, scarves, watches, wallets, whatever. I hated it. *Hated* it. But Seemy pouted and said she really, really wanted to go, so I gave in.

So we walked down to Canal Street, and just like I'd said it would be, the place was filthy with tourists moving slower than snails, loaded down with black plastic bags filled with contraband knockoff purses that they'd bought with thumping hearts in the back rooms of the storefronts that lined the street. And worse, every five seconds some sketchy-looking guy would walk up to us and say in a low voice, "Gucci, Prada, Birkin," wanting us to follow him into those same back rooms to buy crappy knockoffs.

Worse still, it was *hot*, just ridiculously, stupidly HOT.

And then one of those creepy, whispering purse guys actually *touched* my arm to try and get me to stop, and I lost it. I know this city is filled to bursting with people, and sure, you're constantly bumping into each other, but there's an unspoken rule, the reason that people don't go postal and kill each other every other minute. We're crowded, but we don't touch each other unless we have to. Unless someone's on fire or about to step in front of a bus, you can count on the fact that no one is going to reach out and make contact.

But this guy did.

"Don't you touch me!" I screamed in his face. "Do I look like a goddamn tourist to you?" My whole body was shaking, and I thought for a second that I wanted to hit him, that I wanted to punch him right in the nose, and it seemed like such a good idea that I was afraid I might actually do it. So instead I screamed at him again, just screamed right in his face hoping to blow his ears right off his head, and then I grabbed Seemy's arm and pulled her across the street. We got yelled at by the traffic cop and kept walking down one side street and then another until we were on a narrow street shaded by buildings.

"Nan, *stop*!" Seemy was laughing, but I could tell she was freaked out. I still had her wrist, but she stopped walking, dug in her heels, and I let her drag me to a stop. "It's *okay*, Nan, seriously, it's okay."

I didn't even realize I was crying until she handed me the napkin that'd been wrapped around her iced coffee. It was soaked with condensation from the cup, but it felt good on my face.

"It's just . . ." I hiccupped. "It's so *hot*!" And then I turned to look at the window of the restaurant we were standing in front of. It had this giant aquarium filled with gray, bulbous fish with bulging eyes. "And what the hell is wrong with those fish!" They were so slimy and looked so soft, like they were about to fall apart, and all of a sudden I thought I was going to be sick, so I ran into the restaurant next door and asked if I could use the bathroom. I barely even waited for a yes, just bolted for the back of the narrow dining room. I didn't actually throw up in the bathroom, just sat on the can until I stopped crying. I washed my face in the sink, and they were out of paper towels, so I dried it on my shirt.

When I came out, Seemy was sitting at a table. She grabbed my arm and pulled me into the seat next to her, laughing and whispering, "Oh my God, the bathroom's for customers only! I think we *have* to eat here now or they'll call the police!"

"What?" I laughed. "Says who?"

"The owner lady at the front!" Seemy hissed, still cracking up. "Don't look, don't look!"

"Oh my God, you are such a country mouse," I groaned, poking her in the ribs. "All restaurants say that, but they can't, like, *legally* make you eat."

Her face went from happy to glum.

I'd forgotten that she was kind of sensitive about the whole country mouse thing, so I said, "I'm starving, though, so let's eat."

"I thought you just puked."

"Nope, false alarm. What is this place, anyway?"

"Vegetarian dim sum, apparently," she answered coldly, not looking up from the menu.

Of course, when we retold the story to my mom and her mom and whoever else would listen, we left out the country mouse part. We just talked about how we didn't realize that each dim sum item we ordered off the menu came with at least four pieces, so we ordered way too much, and the waiters kept coming out of the kitchen one after another with trays stacked with bamboo steamers filled with delicious dumplings stuffed with mock pork or spinach or banana. They had names like Treasure Boxes and Treasure Balls, and at first when we started eating, we were happy that the waiters kept coming with more and we were laughing at our good food fortune.

But then we started to get full, and they just kept coming with more and more food, and then all of the doughy, fake-meat goodness felt like it had expanded in our stomachs, and by the end we just sat there with glazed eyes, rubbing our bellies and groaning while the waiters laughed at us.

After that we were there at least twice a week for the rest of the summer.

TODAY

Duke's is your typical 1950s-themed diner crammed with calculated nostalgia. Chrome-wrapped countertop, do-wop on the jukebox, waiters in white paper hats, waitresses dressed for a sock hop. The walls are carefully cluttered with tin signs advertising drive-ins, Route 66, and soda fountains. It's way overpriced, but it's open all night and it's close to Saint Marks, so it became our unofficial home base, at least until we found the carriage house. The best part of so many nights with Seemy was rolling into Duke's at three in the morning, both of our moms thinking we were sleeping over at the other's apartment. Toad, the dangling participle, would be there too. We'd be sobering up a little, realizing we hadn't eaten for hours, that our feet hurt and we had to pee, and that we were in danger of getting sleepy.

We'd pool our money and get a giant plate of disco fries, and vanilla Cokes for Seemy and me, and root beer for Toad. I was never so happy as I was sitting in a booth next to Seemy, singing along with the music, teasing Toad. When we left, the sun would just be coming up, and we'd realize we had four or five hours until we could go home to pass out. Toad always offered to let us sleep at his place, but even Seemy thought that was a bad idea. She and I would take these marathon walks all over Manhattan. If we were really tired, we'd get on the L train and sleep as it went from one end of the line to the other.

When I walk into Duke's, Edie is at the far end of the counter. Her hair is shorter, she's gotten coppery highlights, but otherwise she looks the same. She rushes over to greet me.

"OH, HELL NO!" she yells as soon as I sit down at the counter. "Get your ass up off my stool!"

My mouth falls open, but no words come out.

"I swear to God I am so pissed I could kill you, do you know that?" She slaps her hand on the counter in front of me so hard her horn-rimmed glasses fall off her head, skid off the counter, and clack to the ground next to me. I bend over to pick them up. "Leave them!" she yells. "I just want you to get the hell out of here!"

We have the full attention of everyone else in the restaurant now. Dale, the cook, is standing in the entrance to the kitchen, like he's waiting to see if she needs backup.

"I'm . . . I'm sorry," I tell her, slipping off the stool. "I don't know what . . ." I trail off.

She sighs loudly, and then, as if it's against her better judgment, she snaps, "You don't know what?"

My voice is husky, fighting back tears. I keep my eyes on the metal creamer on the counter. "I don't know what happened last night. I don't know why you're mad at me. But I'm sorry. For whatever I did. I'm really, really sorry."

I look up when Edie groans. "You weren't acting like yourself, that's for damn sure."

Everyone is still staring at us. Edie looks around and snaps, "Go back to your pie!"

They do. Then she looks at me and sighs. "Would you get my goddamn glasses, please?"

I bend over to pick them up, and by the time I'm sitting again, she's put a glass of ginger ale in front of me. She leans on the counter, stares at me. "Go on and drink. You look a little green around the gills."

I sip the soda, wait to see if it stays down, and then sip again.

"You weren't yourself last night," Edie says. "I could tell that right off. You and your little friend didn't even say hello to me. You just followed those creeps to a booth in the back. Both of you looking like prom queens from hell." She glowers at me. "I can see you decided to keep the look. What were you two doing with guys like that?"

I look at her blankly. "Guys?"

"You really don't remember?" she asks.

I shake my head.

I don't want to go down this rabbit hole. I don't want to know what happened. But Seemy . . . what about Seemy?

"What guys?" I make myself ask. And then I add hopefully, "Was one of them Toad, that gangly kid we used to come in here with?"

"No, haven't seen that kid for ages. Not sure who these guys were. I'd never seen them before. Seedy-looking dudes, though, older guys. My age. I've never met your mama, but I can bet you she wouldn't want you hanging out with them."

Ask the next question, Nan. "How many?"

"Two guys and the two of you. I kicked you out."

"Why'd you kick us out?"

She narrows her eyes at me, and for a second I think she's going to throw me out all over again. "You came in looking like zombies, your eyes were all messed up, like they are now. Weird dress, messed-up face paint. You looked like you'd been crying, and you went straight to the bathroom. Your little friend followed you. You stayed in there for so long I was about to come look for you, but then you came out and sat down with the two creeps. One of them got up and moved and made sure the two of you were sitting between them. Made sure you couldn't get out. I didn't like that. Not one bit. You and your little friend just sat there staring at the burgers they'd ordered for you. The two guys were having a great time. They were punching each other, really hard, so hard they were bruising, and one of them was bleeding and laughing about it. I was afraid you were going to get hit. They broke a few glasses, hit the booth so hard it cracked away from the wall. Tore the high-quality vinyl seat." She smirks a little. "They scared the other customers. Scared me. I went into the kitchen to get Lenny so he could help me kick them out. I was going to get you girls to stay here so I could call your moms. Lenny told the guys to leave, they refused, but I was ready for that. I showed them I was dialing 911 and that did it. They left. But they took you with them. They slung their arms over you like you were going to prom or something, and I grabbed your friend's arm and said, 'You don't have to go with them,' and she just looked at me and she looked . . . scared, you know? Really scared. And then I tried to grab you, but you

said, 'I'm going with her,' and that was it. You were gone."
She stares blankly at me for a second and then shudders,
takes my glass. "I'm just glad you're okay." She squints at
me. "Though, I'm not sure if you are really okay."

I'm not okay. I grip the edge of the counter to keep from
falling off the stool. I want the spinning to stop. I squeeze
my eyes closed, listen to the water-rushing sound in my
head, punctuated by the sound of Edie dropping my glass
into the sink. The dizziness fades.

"How's your friend?" Edie asks. I have to blink a few
times against the too-bright light. "She okay?"

I close my eyes again. "I don't know."

I'm almost out the door before I turn and ask, "And
you're sure Toad, the kid we used to hang out with, wasn't
with us last night?"

"Sure of it," she says.

REMEMBERING

We met Toad in the dark of the Sunshine Cinema movie theater on Houston Street at a midnight showing of *The Goonies*. It was November, and even though the days were mild, the night air left Seemy and me chilled and reveling in the hot-fire feel of rum slipping down our throats.

"I'm still cold!" Seemy whispered. "Let me put my hands on your belly."

"No way!" I laughed, squirming out of reach and trying to keep my voice down. "You have icicle hands."

"I know!" She was laughing hysterically. "But you're like a big old bear oven and I'm freezing."

I laughed about "bear oven" like it was the funniest thing I'd ever heard, even though it sent pinpricks of hot shame into my throat. Seemy took my laughter as permission, and a second later she had her hands under my shirt, pressing her palms against the soft flesh of my stomach. "Stop it!" I hissed, trying to force a laugh, squirming away so hard that I bumped into the person sitting next to me. I turned to him, pushing Seemy's hands away.

"Sorry," I whispered to him. Then I hissed "Knock it off!" at Seemy and she started pouting.

The kid next to us leaned over and said, "Don't stop on my account."

"Ew, creep!" I said, not even bothering to whisper. I gave him the most evil look I could manage and moved closer to Seemy.

On the movie screen, the Goonies went from the dark of Mikey's attic to the rainy light of day, and the moment the light hit the theater I saw the kid's eyes widen as he saw—really saw—Seemy. The very next second his long arm was stretched across me and he was whispering to her, "I'm Todd. Call me Toad."

Seemy giggled, shook his hand. "Samantha, call me Seemy." Then she nodded toward me and said, "This is my associate, Nan. Call her Nan."

Toad grinned at Seemy, barely glancing at me. "We just

met. Not to be rude, but could that be some fine island rum I smell?"

I stared at him in the dark. He was skinny and tall, a little taller than me even, which, for some reason, pissed me off. He had a big face. A horse face, I thought, or even like an elephant because his nose was kind of big. When he laughed, his lips pulled back and showed all his teeth. They were big too, and kind of came together in a point in his mouth, like the bow of a ship.

"Nan?" Seemy was saying. "Can you?"

I looked over at her. "What?"

She was holding out her hand. "The rum?" she asked.

Toad jiggled the soda cup he was holding out, sloshing the ice around. Great. So now we were going to share with this kid. I handed her the rum, she uncapped it and poured some into the cup.

I sat there waiting for the movie to be over, waiting for this toothy kid to be out of our lives.

But he didn't get out of our lives. He tunneled his way in.

"TOAD!" Seemy and I shrieked, pushing through the crowd on Saint Marks and trying to tackle our new friend Toad as if we hadn't seen him in months, in years, in lifetimes. Really it'd only been a ten-minute pee break in

Starbucks, but we felt alive with the invigorating chill of fall in New York, and with the long, skinny scarves we had wrapped fashionably around our necks, and with the shots of vodka we'd thrown back in the bathroom.

"Relax, girls," Toad said, blushing red as a stoplight, trying to dislodge us from his arms, "you're scaring the tourists."

"Eh, they can screw themselves back to Ohio," Seemy said loud enough to make the people around her look away. She laughed, jumping on Toad's back. He wrapped his arms around her legs and started running down the sidewalk, making them look like a six-foot-something two-headed beast clothed in many shades of black, Seemy's olive green scarf trailing behind them. I was used to their shtick by now, so I didn't walk after them, I just sat down on the closest stoop to pick polish off my fingernails and wait for them to come back.

You could tell he had fallen for Seemy right away, from that first night in the movie theater. They made plans to meet up the next day, and when he saw I was there too, he said, "Oh great, you brought the grim reaper." And Seemy said, "Nanja's my best friend! We do everything together!"

We'd been friends with Toad only a couple weeks, and even though I'd kind of hated him at first, he'd quickly become like an elixir for our rotting friendship. The truth is, the afterglow of our first and only summer together had started to fade. Sometimes I wasn't even sure Seemy liked me anymore. She had friends at her new school, and even though she called them snobs and only hung out with us, I knew she wasn't exactly sitting alone at lunch like I was.

Anyway, even I had to admit that Toad was the pick-me-up our friendship needed.

TODAY

CHAPTER 17

I hate that I need to find that screw-toothed prick.

He'll know where Seemy is, even if he wasn't with us last night. He can tell me that she's okay. I head toward Saint Marks, and I don't even notice that I black out until I come to and realize I'm walking in the wrong direction, the sudden sounds and lights and smells of the city making my bones vibrate like I'm a bell that has just been struck. I stop short and get cursed out by the person behind me, who had to sidestep into a puddle. His umbrella pokes me on the top of my head as he stomps by, and I jerk away and dash across the street and almost get creamed by some shitbox car that sounds like it has a death rattle.

I'm scared.

My hands are fists in my pockets, and I concentrate on the feeling of my nails digging into my palms, picturing the eight crescent-moon indentations they'll leave on my skin.

I think that I might scream, so I duck into the next store I come to. It's a Ricky's, the beauty supply store that clears its shelves for Halloween costumes every year. In the days before Halloween the place is totally mobbed, with a line snaking out the door and down the block. Today, though, it's almost empty. Just a few bargain hunters rifling through the mess that's left after last night.

"I told you!" the woman behind the counter is yelling to someone when I walk in. The store looks like a herd of wildebeests have torn through it. A few rubber masks hang skewered through the eyes on metal wall pegs, wigs lie in open bins tangled with oversize clown glasses and gigantic plastic bras—boobs included. "I told you it wouldn't fit!"

Oh, wait. She's yelling at me. I walk up to the counter. "Excuse me?"

"You're size XL."

"*Dude!*" I object loudly, before lowering my voice so other bargain hunters can't hear me. "You don't have to, like, announce my dress size to the world."

"No size extra large in the Slutty Prom Queen costume!"

"Wha . . . ?" I look down at my dress and then at the rack where she is pointing. There are just a few things left on the rack. Slutty Devil. Slutty Nurse. And, with a tag featuring a girl much skinnier than me, Slutty Prom Queen.

"And you can't return the dress now anyway. You're wearing it."

I pull one of the dresses from the rack and hold it up. "I bought this here?"

"Yes."

"When?"

"Last night! No returns!"

I hold up my hands. "I get it, I'm not going to return the dress that I'm wearing. Can I ask you a question, though?"

She narrows her eyes at me.

"Did I leave my stuff here?"

"No," she says quickly.

"Are you sure? Don't you have a lost-and-found or something?"

She bends over a little, opens up a drawer, and then slams it shut. "Nothing in the lost-and-found."

"Thanks. Was anybody with me? When I came in here on Halloween?"

"Little girl. Bought the same dress." The woman smirks. "Size small."

"Did we try them on? The dresses?"

The woman shrugs.

"Can I check the dressing room? For my stuff?"

I don't wait for an answer; I just duck into the curtained dressing room. The woman calls to me, "Those men you were with weren't good men!"

The dressing room is empty.

My heart thunk-thunk-thunks in my chest as I duck down to look under the bench. "What do you mean?" I ask.

"You didn't want to be with them."

I don't respond. I've found something on the wall. I lay my cheek against it, so my eyes are looking straight across its surface. There's something written there. Something written and wiped away.

HELP US. Then there's a couple letters I can't make out, and then there's a number. My cell phone number. I trace the letters with my fingers. HELP US.

I rest my head against the wall, tears dripping out of my closed eyes.

"Remember," I whisper. I wait for the memories to come. "Remember," I say again. I tap my head against the wall, hoping to jog something loose. Nothing. "Remember," I say louder, and this time my head makes a thunking noise when it hits the wall. "You have to remember!" *Thunk.* "Remember!" *Thunk.* "Remember!" *Thunk.*

"You okay in there?" the woman calls.

My head hurts. This is stupid.

"Okay," I mumble, "okay."

The woman behind the counter calls out to me as I leave, "How is your friend?" but I don't stop. I just push open the doors and walk away as fast as I can.

I have to find Toad.

REMEMBERING

S eemy stretched her bare arms out and held her palms up to the sky, spinning in a circle. "It's crazy warm out! That was the longest winter ever in world history, period, forever, the end."

I smiled sleepily, watched her spin from where I sat on the top step of the fountain in Washington Square Park. She was right, it had been a long winter. Wet and cold and disgusting and never ending. It barely snowed at all, just weeks and weeks of overcast, freezing, windy days and the occasional mix of sleet and freezing rain that made rivers and lakes of slush in the streets.

It was like the weather had tried its best to scrub out

all memory of me and Seemy's summer together, until all I felt when I looked at her was cold. Our friendship had been shoved into the margins since Christmas. On weeknights we both had to be home by seven, and to Seemy that meant we had to spend the few hours of freedom we had freezing our asses off on Saint Marks Place with Toad, maybe drinking if she had anything, but mostly just wandering from store to store, coffee shop to coffee shop, never inside long enough to really warm up. And even though she complained about the cold outside, she couldn't stand to be indoors. "If we were upstate," she'd say, "we'd be out hiking in the woods right now." She'd go off on how the city was unnatural, on how it felt like we were all going to snap our tethers to Mother Nature and go flying off into the universe. Toad would say, "Yeah, man, you're right." But he'd say that for anything Seemy said.

I barely ever saw her on weekdays anymore. Weekends I'd still go along with it, mostly because I didn't have anyone else to hang out with. My old friends from school didn't want anything to do with me. And I acted like I didn't want anything to do with them.

But then there was a Tuesday in March, the first really warm day of spring, when Seemy called me after school and said we should meet up, and the air was so warm and it felt like the tiniest whisper of summer and I couldn't say no.

There was hope in the air. The sun was so warm I dozed off for a second, woke up when Seemy screeched, "TOAD!" and I watched her leap up and try to climb him like a bean stalk. He was smiling this goofy, big-toothed smile, and his nasty black cargo pants were paired with a clean olive green T-shirt, no jacket. His long, pale arms glowed in the sunlight like the skin under a picked scab.

"Let's go," Toad said, balancing Seemy on his back. "I have someplace special to take you guys. Even *you*, grumpy face." He nodded to me with a snaggletoothed grin.

"Where, where, where?" Seemy squealed, wiggling down and then hopping in a circle around him.

"It's a surprise," he said, "a *good* surprise." He looked genuinely excited, but he jutted his chin out a little when he looked to see if I'd follow, like he expected me to rain on his parade.

"Let's go," I said, stepping off the fountain.

We walked for a while, all the way up University to Union Square, where we pooled our money to buy apple cider doughnuts at the farmer's market. We kept heading north and then turned left on Nineteenth Street. By this time we were thirsty, so we used Seemy's credit card to buy the first iced coffees of summer, even though the sun was getting low and the air was starting to chill so much I kept having to switch hands to keep my fingers from going numb. I felt this sort of hope for the future. It was nice to be walking along with two friends in the almost-warm air, eating doughnuts and drinking iced coffee and joking and teasing and yelling and scaring the other pedestrians.

We walked past Seventh Avenue, then Eighth, and then the buildings started to get nicer. There were a lot of brownstones with huge windows, giving us glimpses of their fancy interiors.

"Toad," Seemy asked, "are you about to tell us that you're secretly rich or something?"

"Nope, even better," Toad said, then he laughed. "Well, maybe not better, but almost as good."

He stopped walking suddenly at the mouth of a narrow alley between two brownstones. He looked quickly around, then hurried down the alley, turning around and grinning, whispering, "Come on!" Seemy grabbed my hand, pulled me in after her. At the end of the alley was a black iron gate, and beyond that there was a falling-apart tiny brick house surrounded by overgrown grass and mud. The house had huge black double doors that took up almost the whole front of it, and a couple little windows with white sills above.

We stood side by side, our fingers hooked in the iron gate, staring at it.

Seemy said, "It's like a real house. A house that can take a deep breath."

You don't see a lot of freestanding houses in New York City. Even the fancy buildings share walls with their neighbors. But this place, this place actually had space, and Seemy was right, seeing it sitting there alone in the swampy yard made you want to take a deep breath.

"It's a carriage house, used to be a horse hotel for rich people," Toad said proudly. "They were going to renovate it and turn it into a house for some rich dude, but he ran out of money. My uncle was on the construction crew and told me about it. It's totally empty. It's like . . . ours."

Seemy looked at him with such wonder that I got a tinge of jealousy. "Ours, Toad, really?" she asked. I bit my tongue, wanting to say, *No, actually, it's not ours at all. Not even a little bit.* But they both looked so happy I didn't say a thing.

Toad scaled the iron gate, long monkey limbs making it easy work. Seemy looked at me expectantly and I tried to smile while bending over so she could climb up on my back and get high enough for Toad to pull her over. Then they both started walking toward the carriage house, and Seemy called over her shoulder, "Nan, come on!"

And I was standing alone on the other side of the gate, so I did what she said.

The front lawn was soaked and spongy from the spring rains, and our feet got stuck and made loud slurping noises as we pulled them free. Seemy sank almost to her knees right before we got to the rotting front steps, and Toad and I had to pull her out. We laughed so hard I thought we might die, and we feverishly shushed each other and started laughing all over again.

It took all three of us to pull open one side of the double doors.

"Oh my gosh, horse stalls!" Seemy squealed when we got inside. Toad took out a flashlight and shone it around. He had come prepared. There were three stalls on either side of the stone walkway that ran down the middle of the house.

"I love it." Seemy sighed. "Even if it does smell like horse poop. Is there a hayloft?" she asked, clapping her hands as she ran to the back of the carriage house, where a wooden ladder reached into a dark hole in the ceiling.

"Yeah, but it's treacherous." Toad shone his flashlight at the holes in the ceiling. "There's rats up there, too."

"We can stay down here then," Seemy said, pirouetting her way back to us and then grabbing us both in a hug. "This place is awesome."

TODAY

I find Toad hunched under an awning on Saint Mark's, hands cupped around a take-out cup of coffee. He looks the same. Same stupid pants. Maybe a little skinnier.

"Hey, Toad."

He looks at me, startled, then turns away. "What do you want?" He asks, his back toward me.

I hate that he makes me nervous. I step under the awning. "Been a long time."

He snorts, making a big show of turning to face me. "Has it?"

"How are you?"

He ignores my question. "Go to hell, Nanja."

He throws his half-drunk coffee into the gutter and starts walking, pulling his head down, like a turtle, into his collar. I walk after him. "Will you wait up, please? Toad, just hold on!"

He spins around so quickly that I run into him, and he pops his chest forward, knocking me back a little. I catch my balance. "What?" he snaps, rain falling down his face.

"Nothing . . . ," I falter. "So . . . have you seen Seemy?"

He sneers at me, laughs a wide-mouthed laugh that sends rain in a stream off his top lip. "Seemy? Why do you care? I thought you rehabbed us right out of your life."

"Come on . . ."

"Come on what?" His voice cracks. "Step thirteen, cut the loser dead weight from your life even if it's your best friend, you can't give a shit about them anymore no matter what happens to them." He sniffs loudly, wipes angrily at his eyes, and I realize it's not just rain, he's actually crying. "Damn it!" He starts walking quickly away.

"Toad, what are you talking about?" I splash after him and he swings around.

"I'm talking about the fact that I haven't seen Seemy in weeks! And I don't know where she is, and her parents won't talk to me! Do you know the things that could have happened to her? Do you know the kind of people she started hanging out with when you left?"

"You mean like you?" I yell back at him.

He looks like he wants to laugh, but instead he yells, "Me? You think I'm a problem? You have *no idea*! *NO IDEA!*"

And then he says, "Where did you go? Just now? You just, like, went blank, right in front of me." He steps closer to me, grabs my chin, and looks into my eyes. When he lets go, he yells, "I don't freaking believe you! You're using! You ditch us because we're stupid losers, and then you go and . . ." He makes a sound that I think is supposed to be laughter. "You're unbelievable."

"I'm worried about her, Toad. I feel like . . ." My stomach heaves and I have to stop, take a deep breath before I continue. "I feel like something bad happened to her."

Toad huffs, shakes his head. He looks suddenly exhausted. "Well, welcome to my world. I've been worried about her for weeks. I don't know what to tell you."

"Do you know where to find her?"

"Have you heard anything I've said?" he snaps. "I *can't* find her!"

"But . . . maybe there's someplace you guys used to hang out—"

"Oh, what? Like the carriage house? You don't think I've checked there?" He looks like he wants to rip my head off. "Why'd you have to stop hanging out with her, Nan?

Why would you do that? Was your stupid Nanapocalypse really that bad that you would ditch your best friend?"

"I had to."

"You left her alone!" he yells.

"I didn't leave her alone!" I scream at him. "I left her with you!"

"Well," he says, raising his hands and dropping them again, "I wasn't enough to keep her." He sneers at me. "Go screw yourself, Nan. She never loved either of us. You were just smart enough to stop trying to change her mind."

REMEMBERING

The night of the Nanapocalypse, I wasn't even supposed to go out, which was fine with me.

I was all set to stay home with the Tick and watch movies, but the gallery opening Mom was going to got canceled, so she ended up coming home early and she plopped down on the couch to watch movies with us, and even though I was all snuggled up under a blanket on the big chair with the Tick, I couldn't stand to be in the same room with her.

In the past week she'd accused me of stealing a ten-dollar bill from her wallet (which I did), yanked the lock out of my bedroom door because I went into my bedroom without letting her smell my breath after being out with Seemy, and told me if I put one more hole in my face she was putting me under house arrest.

There was no way I could breathe the same air as her for a whole Saturday night.

So I bailed, and even though she told me I couldn't, I just walked right out. It was either let me walk out or get in my way, and I knew she didn't want to have that kind of fight in front of the Tick.

I got into the elevator and I was shaking, and I started crying because things were so bad with my mom and I didn't know how they had gotten that way but I knew it was my fault.

The thing was, I didn't really want to meet up with Seemy. I just didn't have anywhere else to go. She and Toad were coming out of the alley that led to the carriage house when I turned the corner, and Seemy squealed so loud my heart leaped and she came running and jumped into my arms and I knew that was right where I was supposed to be.

She jumped off of me and clapped her hands like a little kid. "I'm so glad you came, Nanja! I thought you had to babysit!"

I glanced uneasily at Toad. He sighed, cracked his knuckles. "Let's walk," he said. He was always worried one of the neighbors would notice us coming and going from the carriage house. He walked ahead of us and after a dozen yards called over his shoulder, "So, what are we doing? I'm bored."

Seemy ran to catch up with him, reaching back to pull me along. "Me too! Let's do something! What are we going to do?"

Her energy was usually infectious, it was usually enough to make me excited for a night of aimless wandering and pointed drinking, but that night the thought made me weary. I pushed the feeling down until it was just a black seed in my stomach.

"Let's party," Toad said, looking right at me.

"Well, *duh*!" Seemy laughed. "Of course we're going to party! Right, Nan?"

A couple of hours later it was dark out and it'd gotten cold, but it was all right because I couldn't feel my skin. We'd smoked some, drunk some, and we were running down the street, I'm not sure to where. My feet felt springy, like rubber, like I was bouncing as I ran. Felt wonderful.

I would have been good stopping, going someplace to ride it out, but Seemy and Toad wanted to keep going, so we did.

After that it's a little fuzzy. We drank at the carriage house for a while. And then I think we were at McDonald's.

And then maybe the movies. And Toad kept cheering me on, being really cool to me, wrapping his arm around me, helping me drink more when I couldn't lift the bottle.

And then I was looking at our apartment building, except it was on its side, and it was melting away in the rain. Someone was yelling at me. They were being really, really mean. I was throwing up, and it was getting all over me. Chuck was there. He was upside down, looking at me, and then he was picking me up, and then he was right side up and so was our apartment building.

When they redid the building, the owners put one of those flat, backless modern couches in the lobby. Chuck laid me down on it, and I watched the room spin as he called up to our apartment. Then my mom was there. And Chuck wanted to carry me upstairs, but she did it herself. And I felt so small in her arms, like a little baby, and then I threw up again.

Mom sat with me all night, helping me throw up, keeping me on my stomach, waking me up every five minutes to make sure I didn't pass out and die. She said she kept the phone next to her because she thought she'd have to dial 911.

By morning I was in Mom's bed, because at some point in the night I threw up and peed myself at the same time. She'd helped me into the shower, got herself soaked reaching in to wash my hair. I had to sit down, was still too dizzy to stand. The Tick was supposed to be asleep, but I don't see how he could have slept through the commotion. He appeared in the bathroom doorway, rubbing his eyes, blinking at the light, asking Mom if I was okay. Her voice was high pitched, overly reassuring. "Just go back to bed, I'll come tuck you in in a minute. Nan has a tummy ache."

She wrapped me in a towel, brought me to her room, and laid a sheet down on top of her covers, thin protection in case I got sick again. Over me she pulled the blanket we use when we're watching movies on the couch. She sat next to me, watching while I slept.

I woke up when I heard the front door click shut. It was sunny. Morning time. There was a note by the bed: JUST DOWNSTAIRS GIVING THE TICK TO HIS DAD, BACK IN A MINUTE. I had to pee, so I swung my legs over the side of the bed and then sat there for a minute, feeling like I was going to puke again. Then I slid off the bed, not bothering with the towel because I could tell I was *definitely* going to puke again. But I didn't just puke. I had really superbad diarrhea. So I sat on the toilet and hugged the trash can between my knees and wished not that I were dead, but that it were days and weeks and months and years away from this moment.

I decided to shower again, reached over in our tiny

bathroom and turned on the water, waited till it was hot and then got in. But I was still shaky, and the floor in the shower was slick, and I slipped almost immediately and fell forward and cracked my head against a broken piece of tile. When Mom came and found me and saw the blood all over me and swirling down the drain, she thought I had slit my own throat or something.

A couple of days after that, when I was home from the hospital for just long enough to pack a bag, I sneaked into the closet and called Seemy for the first time.

"They're sending you to *rehab*?" She screeched into the phone.

"It's not really rehab," I told her, "it's like some sort of—"

"Oh my God, you're, like, practically the sober one out of all of us!" I heard her lower the phone and say, "Toad! Nanja's going to rehab!" Then she said to me, "That's too funny, girl, I can't believe it. How long are you going for? When do you come back? Can we come visit? Oh my God, it'd be really funny to visit you in rehab. We'll make ourselves T-shirts, 'Nan went to rehab and all I got was this—'"

I hung up on her.

TODAY

I don't know where else to go. I don't know how to find Seemy. I don't know what to do.

So I go home.

It's past four when I get back to my apartment building, and between the clouds and the rain it's starting to get dark already.

"Seta get back?" I ask Chuck. He nods and pulls a spare set of keys to our apartment from his top drawer.

"You don't look well, Nan," he says.

"I'm not," I tell him, walking to elevators.

I hear his chair squeak as he gets up, and a moment later

he's next to me. "When's your mother coming home? Do you want me to call her?"

I jab at the elevator call button again. "No. I'm fine. Just a touch of the flu or something."

"You're shaking," he says, taking my hand as I reach for the button again. I pull my hand away.

"I'm just cold," I snap.

"It's sixty degrees out," he shoots back.

I blink at him. The elevator doors open, and I get in and press the door button. "I'm fine," I tell him as the doors close.

The familiar sound of the locks on our apartment door clicking into place behind me is so reassuring, my eyes go blurry with tears. I move quickly through the apartment, turning on all the lights and cranking up the heat. Everything looks the way it should look, but nothing feels the way it should feel. I want the sight of my cereal bowl in the sink and the Tick's Legos on the coffee table to comfort me with their sameness, but they look like scenes from someone else's life. I want, more than anything, to feel okay again, to have this terrible feeling inside me go away.

I'm going to call Mom and I'm going to tell her everything. Even the familiar sound of her disappointment would be a comfort. She can be as disappointed as she wants to be, I don't care—I just want her to help me find Seemy.

I go into the bathroom first, and that's where I find my backpack.

It's just lying in the middle of the fuzzy purple bathmat, where I always drop it when I rush in after school to pee. It feels like so long ago that finding it was the most important thing in the world to me.

I rip open the main part of the backpack and then drop it to the floor. My hair, a rainbow rat's nest, spills out onto the floor. I reach down, touch it lightly with my fingertips. It feels like me, only less alive.

I find my ID in the front pocket. The picture on it was taken the first day at my new school. I sit on the edge of the tub and stare at it, flipping it over and over in my hands.

REMEMBERING

The summer after the Nanapocalypse passed in a stream of too-hot days with too much sun and not enough air-conditioning. I had a summer cold that kept coming back, and I alternated a million times a day between sweating from the weather when I was outside, sweating from a fever when I was inside, and shivering when the fever broke, whether I was outside or in. Mom said it was my body adjusting, cleaning itself out. It made me think that every time I sneezed or coughed up a chunk of something gross, a piece of the old me was flying out of my body. I was glad to see it go. Mom would look into my eyes, and it felt like she was looking way down into my guts to see how much of the dark stuff was left.

The sickness made the whole summer surreal. Like I was watching myself through mottled glass that would catch the sun and burn my eyes without warning. Nothing I ate could get rid of the taste of antibiotics. Back when I was hanging out with Seemy, I never really cared if we drank or if we didn't. What I wanted was to hang out with her. I didn't have that thing she had, the thing that made her make smacking noises with her tongue against the roof of her mouth, the thing that made her grumble, "I'm thirsty." Seemy knew I didn't want it like she wanted it, and I think she started to hate me because she thought I was judging her, and she was right. "It seems to me," one of my counselors said to me, "you don't have a drinking problem, you have a bad-choices problem."

Now I wanted to drink something that would burn the taste out of my mouth, set fire to my throat, singe my insides clean.

"New school, new you!" Mom chirped at me whenever the subject of my new school came up. She should know that she's not a woman who can chirp convincingly. She's like me. Wide shouldered and barrel chested and made to growl. Chirping makes her sound frantic, like she's losing her grip on her sanity. *New school, new you.* She would say it like it was a good thing, a fantastic opportunity, like I had made a really great choice, instead of having no choice at all.

I didn't want a new school. I wanted to go back to my old school, but they wouldn't have me. Too many unexcused absences last year. Dr. Friedman even wrote a letter on my behalf, but it didn't make a difference. They wanted me out. *New school, new you.* I had no choice in the "new school" part, but the "new you" part, that's where I could make my stand.

Over the summer Mom and I had constant minisqualls about my appearance that left us both flushed and quiet, neither of us wanting to push the subject for fear of our fragile peace cracking in half. The fissures were there, though, and the night before school started, Mom stuck a fingernail into the biggest one and gave it a wiggle.

"So, are you all ready for school?" She was sitting crosslegged on my bed, watching me comb out my hair after my shower.

I gave her reflection in the mirror a halfhearted shrug. "I guess." I studied the thick stripe of purple that ran from the crown of my head down to where my hair ended below my shoulders. It was a supervised dye job. Mom said my hair could be a maximum of two colors. She took out the student handbook for my new school and showed me the section about "Distracting Clothing or Appearance." She said it meant I couldn't go to school with my hair eight different colors. And that I had to take out my lip ring and my eyebrow ring and my tongue ring. Even though she tried not to gloat, I could tell she was happy. Over the summer I kept catching her glowering at my hair, her eyes flicking from color to color, her lips pressed together.

For my two colors, I chose to keep it all black, except for the one stripe of purple.

"What do you think you're going to wear?" she asked, her voice thick with forced casualness.

We looked at each other for a long moment in the mirror. I finally nodded to the futon in the corner, the one Seemy and I had covered completely in duct tape on a freezing cold day last winter. On the chair was a pile of clothing. My usual. A pair of new black leggings, a black A-line lace skirt. A couple of black T-shirts. It was still hot out. On the floor next to the chair were my boots, freshly polished for the occasion, with new purple laces I had to special-order online, still in the package, waiting to be threaded through.

Mom didn't get up, but she stared across the room at the clothes like she was fighting the urge to jump up and stomp on them. She pursed her lips. "I don't really think—"

"It doesn't matter what you think." I swung around, my anger so hot and so sudden that I made myself lean back against my bureau to keep from throwing my hairbrush against the wall. I clutched it to the towel around my chest, my wrists crossed, feeling the double echo of my racing pulse against my heartbeat.

All I could think was, *Stop-stop-stop. We have to stop. We're going to break everything.*

But Mom was up off the bed. She kept her distance, crossing her arms in front of her, glaring at me, rocking slightly from side to side. "Actually, it does matter what I think."

Anger prickled up the back of my neck. "Mom . . . don't."

"Don't what?" she asked, but from the look on her face she knew exactly what I was talking about.

"I've been doing really well all summer. You know that."

She nodded but wouldn't look at me. "I know. But you're actually still on probation with me."

"Oh really?" I was raising my voice now. "I'm on probation? That's what you call it? Because it feels to me like I'm still behind bars."

"Actually—"

"Stop saying 'actually'!" I yelled, and I could see we were both scared because finally one of us was yelling and it felt like something was being ripped down the middle between us. "You don't own me, Mom."

"ACTUALLY, I do!" she yelled.

I couldn't believe how much it hurt to hate someone you love.

"No, you don't," I said quietly, trying to keep from crying. "Just because I messed up doesn't mean I turned my soul over to you. It doesn't mean you get to take away every freedom I've ever had."

"Nan," she said quietly. "You didn't start dressing this way until you started to get in trouble. How am I to think there's not a connection?"

"*Mom*, I'm not going to fall off the wagon because I have purple hair and combat boots. I'm going to jump off the goddamn wagon because you won't let me be myself!"

She walked over to the duct-tape chair and started picking up the clothes, then held them out and made a face like she was trying to stifle a burp. "Can we at least agree on a shirt without holes in it?" She put the stuff down, walked over to my closet, and opened the door.

"Mom, no!" I was in front of her, holding the door closed with one hand, trying to keep my towel on with the other. The thought of her rifling through my closet made my blood boil. "Get out of my room! You have to trust me to be able to at least pick out my own goddamn clothes!"

"Well, I don't!" she yelled in my face, so close I could see the gray of the back tooth she needed to get pulled.

"Well, then that's your problem," I said quietly.

"Because I don't know what else I can do to show you that I've changed."

Mom raised her eyebrows and looked pointedly at the closed closet door and then back at me.

"Wow," I whispered, disappointment choking my voice. "I guess . . . I guess if that's what it takes." I opened the closet door and stepped back. "Have at it. Pick whatever you want. I'll wear it."

"Nan . . ." For some reason Mom sounded even more disappointed than me, like she was hoping I'd fight her on this.

"What?" I sat down on the bed. "If this is what it takes for you to trust me, then fine." She started to respond, but I cut her off. "Because I can't take you looking at me like that anymore, Mom. You make me feel like I'm walking on ice and you're just waiting for me to fall through. Like you *know* I'm going to fall through and you're just deciding if you're going to throw me a rope. So what will it be? Pigtails and overalls? What sort of outfit says 'not a drunk screwup' to you? What sort of outfit will make you love me again?"

I burst into tears. And Mom did too, and then she was hugging me and I was hugging her and trying to hold my towel up at the same time.

The next day she let me walk out of the house in the morning in my favorite blacks; she even helped me put the new laces in my boots. She took a first-day-of-school picture of the Tick and me out on the fire escape, him standing in front of me, grinning his gap-toothed smile, me pretending to have him in a headlock, my long hair hanging over him.

My new school was fine. "It's just a school, I don't know," I said to Mom that night when she pressed me for details. "No, I didn't really talk to anyone." I could see her bite back a response, thinking I was clomping around school in my boots with my scary clothes and a *Don't mess with me* look on my face, that it was my fault that nobody talked to me, that I was scaring them off on purpose. Like I was a skunk with my own back-off stench, the kind that went straight to the back of your throat and made you gag.

She was right.

TODAY

D r. Friedman said that life is full of crossroads; full of moments when you decide to go one way or another. She said I *knew* how to make good decisions. I made them every day. Don't cross the street when there's a bus coming. Don't pick up a hot pan with your bare hands. She said I just had to use those same decision-making smarts when it came to the other parts of my life.

Is this what she meant?

Did she mean that when I am here, sitting on the edge of the tub, wondering what to do next, there is a right answer and a wrong answer? Did she think that I would know which is which?

I am ashamed at what I am thinking.

Because as I flip my ID over and over in my fingers, I am thinking how I could just neatly trim up my hair and make it look like I cut it short on purpose. I could go to Sephora and get someone there to help me figure out what would get this makeup off. I could stuff this dress down the garbage chute.

I could pretend like this morning never happened.

I could stop looking for answers. I could stop looking for Seemy.

But I won't. I'm going to call Mom and she'll come back home and we'll call the police together. And I'm going to tell them most everything. And they're going to help me find out that Seemy's okay.

I'm just going to take a shower first.

That's not the wrong thing to do, right?

And it's not like I'll be lying about last night, because I don't remember anything anyway. I just don't want her to come home and take one look at me and think that I look like a freak. I want to be clean. Put together. I'll dig out a pair of normal-looking jeans and a sweater from my closet. I'll wear a hat. And the set of pearl earrings that Dad gave me, when we all thought I'd be wearing them to their wedding.

I turn the shower on and take the MTA coat off. I

start to pull the pink plastic dress off over my head, but it starts to rip and I just tear the whole thing off my body and throw it against the bathroom door. I peel off my yoga pants, my underwear, and stand naked in front of the mirror.

Painted face. Chopped-up hair. Words scrawled on my chest. Cuts on my arm. They all add up to an answer that I don't want to hear.

I brush my teeth while the shower heats up. Then I get in.

For a long time I just stand with my eyes closed, my head tipped forward so the water hits the top of my head, the soft spot I was terrified of touching on the Tick until he was well past two, wondering at the evil and cunning of a God that would put a baby's kill switch on top of their heavenly-smelling head.

I start to get dizzy, my body sways so far forward I have to touch the slick tiles to steady myself. I flash back to the morning after the Nanapocalypse, of the feeling of the bathtub slipping out from under me, of the tile wall rushing forward and smacking me in the head. I lower myself so I'm sitting; the water is hitting me in the face. I hold my hands out in front of me, palms up, fingers spread. I run my soapy hands over my breasts, my stomach, my back, my butt, down my legs. I lift my feet to scrub them and discover a few shallow slashes on their soles, a bruise in the middle of one heel. From running up the subway stairs, I guess.

I use the facecloth everywhere, even on my head, scrubbing hard until it feels like a layer of gritty skin has been rubbed off and the water is making closer contact with my brain. I scrub my face, checking the washcloth again and again when I see more of the white paint being wiped off.

When I turn off the shower, I feel clean, like my outside is washed, and my insides, too. I reach out of the shower, grab a towel, and wrap it around myself. Next step will be to fix my hair. And then call Mom.

I use my palm to wipe the steam off the bathroom mirror so I can study my hair, figure out how to make it look not so much like an attack but a purposeful makeover. A lot of the face makeup has come off, but not quite all of it. I blink at myself in the mirror, unsure how to make myself look like someone my mother would want to claim as her own. I give up after a few minutes.

I leave the bathroom and go into my bedroom to charge my phone. I'm going to call Mom. She'll come home and she'll help me. I plug my phone into the charger on top of my record player by my bed and wait for it to reset.

When it does, I hear the familiar chime indicating that I have messages.

I have to bend down to listen, since the cord is so short. Two messages, one new, one old.

The new one is from Mom: "Hi Nan, it's Mom. Just calling to see how it's going, and to remind you to make sure the door is double locked before you go to bed. Love you!"

The next shows I listened to it yesterday at 4 p.m. "Nan. It's Seemy. Hey, can you meet me? I'm at the park by my house." I hear people talking in the background. Seemy talks louder. "We're going to have SO much fun, you HAVE to come! Come right now, okay? I'll see you soon!" Before the message ends, I hear Seemy talking to someone. "She'll come, I'm sure of it."

It's past five now.

I stay sitting on my floor, stare out the window into the city-light darkness.

Now is when I should call Mom. The phone is almost charged. And even if it weren't, I could call her from the lobby downstairs. That's what I should do. That is the path to take at the crossroads.

If I call Mom, she'll call the police and race home in a borrowed car. The police will be here when she gets here, or maybe they'll have taken me to the hospital already. They'll question me while I'm in the hospital bed, ask me questions I can't answer. They'll glance at each other, use their police telepathy to tell each other I'm useless. That I'm lying or that I've fried my brain so badly I truly can't remember. Mom will burst into the room and say, *Oh, Nan!* And then she'll start crying. And then she and the police officers will go out into the hall and she'll say, *I just don't know what else to do.* And they'll say, *You've done your best, ma'am, some kids just can't be saved.* And they'll keep asking me what happened to Seemy and I won't be able to tell them and I'll never ever see her again.

But if instead . . .

If I go to Twee park by Seemy's house, maybe I will remember. Maybe I will know where to find her, and when I find her, I'll see she's really okay. Then we can talk about everything that's happened. We'll hug. She'll smell like she always smells. She'll link her arm through mine and we'll walk around the city all night. We'll cry and say our sorries. And tomorrow I will go to school and will buzz all day with the glory of no sleep and friends found again. I will bring my ID to school. Sheila will give me a candy from the stash in her drawer. Maybe I will smile at someone, make a new friend, bringing my total to two. Mom will come home. Dad will call and offer to drive Tick home. Mom will say no, that's okay, we'll come get him. Mom and I will take the train into Greenpoint and then all of us will go out for pierogies. Mom and Dad will watch each other while we eat. They'll walk ahead of us on the way back to Dad's apartment. Tick and I will trail behind. Maybe I'll sling him up on my back and carry him. Maybe we'll stop at the Thing, his favorite junk store, and look at records. Maybe while we're in there, Mom and Dad will keep walking ahead of us and they'll hold hands, and we'll have to run to catch up, and when we do, they'll turn and look at us with delighted surprise, like they forgot we were there.

Sitting down in the comfort of my bedroom, still warm from the shower, I start to feel sleepy. My eyelids start to flutter closed. I feel my hands go limp and fall to the floor. I'll close my eyes just for a few minutes, just until my cell phone is charged and I can bring it with me to the park to find Seemy.

Just for a few minutes.

REMEMBERING

A week after my welcome-home-from-rehab dinner, a week of me feeling completely and utterly lost and alone and realizing that if I didn't have Seemy, I didn't have anyone, she called and asked if she could come over. Mom still had my cell phone at that point, and if I hadn't happened to wander into her studio the moment Seemy called, I'm not sure she would have told me.

I could tell who it was right away by the way Mom's shoulder blades cinched together. I watched Mom stand at her canvas, paintbrush in one hand, phone in the other, a bright rectangle of light coming through the window.

"I don't know, Samantha," Mom was saying. She listened for a moment. "I'm sorry you feel that way, but Nan needs to do what's best for her right now. She told me about your showing up drunk at Duke's."

I groaned, and Mom looked at me, startled.

"It's really up to Nan." She held the phone away from her mouth and asked, "Nan, do you want Seemy to come over? She wants to talk."

Right at that moment there was nothing, *nothing*, that made me angrier than having my mother act like she knew anything about my life. Like she had any right to be on the phone with my best friend, playing gatekeeper, delighting in the fact that after months of me shutting her out, she had forced her way into control. I didn't care that I'd messed up, that I'd done wrong. She had no right.

I wanted to scream at her, I wanted to scream loud enough to break all the windows in her studio. But I remembered the way she'd looked at me when I woke up in the hospital. How scared she looked. How heartbroken. I did that to her. I broke her heart.

So I just nodded and said, "Sure, I'll see her."

Mom watched me for a moment, like she hoped if she stared at me long enough, I'd change my mind. Finally she said to Seemy, "You can come for a few minutes. That's it."

When she got off the phone, Mom put her hands on her hips and said, as if we were friends, as if we were commiserating, "I can't believe she had the nerve to call. After what she did to you at Duke's."

"I shouldn't have told you about that," I said quietly.

"Why? I'm glad you did. I'm glad you felt you could be honest with me."

"Yeah, but that shouldn't mean . . ." I cleared my throat, choosing my words carefully as Mom watched me squirm. "It shouldn't mean you can hold it over my head forever. If I want to be friends with her, I'll be friends with her. Doesn't mean I'm going to drink again."

"Well." Mom picked up her paintbrush. "I don't know how you'll be friends with her, then, because you told me yourself that drinking is all she wants to do."

I groaned and turned to walk out of the room. "I shouldn't have told you that."

"Well, you did!" Mom called after me.

Seemy was wearing a sundress when she got to our door, and I realized it was May, almost summer, almost a year anniversary of our friendship.

"Mom," I finally said, when it became abundantly clear she wanted to stand and listen to Seemy and me as we talked at the kitchen table. "Can you . . ."

"Five minutes, Samantha," Mom said to Seemy, and then she went into her bedroom, leaving the door open.

Seemy rolled her eyes and took a sip of iced coffee. She'd brought me over one too. A peace offering, I guess. "Wow, she still *really* doesn't like me."

I shrugged, pressing my fingertips into the condensation on the side of the coffee cup.

"I mean, it's not like I'm the one that got you sent to rehab, right?" Seemy sipped and watched me for my reaction. "I mean, you did that all on your own."

I looked up at her and said sharply, "She knows that. I know that."

Seemy shook the ice in her drink. "Ah, taking responsibility, right? That's a big thing for you now."

I leaned back in my chair, crossed my arms over my chest. "I guess. Yeah, it is."

Seemy looked at me for a long moment and then said, "You know, you presented yourself under false pretenses." She looked really satisfied with herself.

"What do you mean?"

She raised her eyebrows. "You know what I mean. That day in the park, the day we met. You acted like you were this badass New Yorker, and you're not."

"I never pretended anything."

Seemy laughed. "Oh really? You never pretended like you liked to party? You never pretended that you were *so goth* and *so alternative* and *so punk rock*? You're a faker, Nan."

You're like a little prude in the shape of the Big Bad Wolf."

I sipped my iced coffee, hoping to swallow down the lump in my throat.

Seemy grinned and leaned forward. "So what, are we not allowed to hang out anymore? I thought we could, as long as you didn't drink."

I tried not to roll my eyes. "Yeah, but Seemy . . . that doesn't mean you drink and I don't. Doesn't mean I want to show up somewhere and have you be loaded."

"So drink," she whispered to me, still leaning forward. "It'll make this whole thing much easier."

I snorted. "I don't do that anymore."

Seemy threw up her hands, picked up her sunglasses, and pushed them back in her hair like a headband. "I don't know what I'm supposed to do, Nan. Because you don't drink now, I'm supposed to stop too?"

I hesitated before answering. "Wouldn't kill you to cut down a little."

"Get over yourself, Nan. I'm not like you. I'm not going to rehab. Jesus, what a joke! You barely drank, you know that, right? You're a goddamn woolly mammoth, but you're a total lightweight. It's like you thought you were going to rehab for me and Toad, too. It doesn't work that way, Nan. We like our life the way it is. We don't want it to change."

"But I've changed."

"No you haven't!" she said, trying to keep her voice down. "You look the same to me! If you're so different, why don't you ditch your stupid costumes? Why don't you wash all that rainbow crap out of your hair? You're not fooling anyone anymore, especially now that you're Miss Sobriety. Get yourself a pair of sensible *slacks* and be done with it!"

"I changed on the inside, Seemy."

She laughed. "Right. Whatever. Look, I still want to be friends with you, but I'm not going to change who I am. I, unlike you, *like* who I am. I don't spend all my time hating myself."

"I don't know if I can be friends with you anymore, then."

Her tears surprised me. "You're serious? You're going to dump me because I'm not a total stuck up prude?"

"I can't go back to that life, Seemy."

"What life?" she snapped. "We weren't *doing* anything that bad, Nan! Jesus, you act as if we were doing smack under the Brooklyn Bridge! We drank a little. Got caught. It's called being an American teenager, Nan, it's not this big drama you're making it out to be. Jesus, what the hell did you tell those people at rehab? They must have fallen asleep in group therapy whenever you spoke because your *problems* are so fricking vanilla compared to . . ." She stopped.

"Compared to what?"

She fiddled with her sunglasses again and stood up. "Nothing. Forget it. I'll see you around. Maybe I can schedule a sober day into my schedule and we can hang out." Then, loudly, she said, "Your mom can piss-test me if she wants to."

"Seemy . . ." I was too drained to stand up, but I reached out for her.

"I'll see you around, Nan."

Except she didn't. That was in May. Almost six months ago. And I hadn't seen her since.

TODAY

I wake up laughing and calling out, *Hellooooo!* Seemy is standing on a bench in the park by her house on Halloween, jumping up and down and waving at me as I come through the gate, and she looks so much like herself, so much like I remember, I get a lump in my throat and I laugh it away. I know it's been months, but I run to her and she leaps into my arms and just the familiar feel of her body makes me laugh again and I spin her around and the trees and the bench and the trash can blur as we go around and around. *Tree bench trash tree bench trash tree bench trash men.* I gasp in alarm and stop spinning. Two men, stepping out from behind a cluster of trees. *Who are they?* I ask her, and she wiggles free. *My friends,* she says. *They're my new friends.*

I wake up running and crying and I've got Seemy by the wrist and we're both in pink prom dresses and I'm yanking her along with me and I'm shoving clowns and monsters and zombies and French maids out of our way and then we break through the crowd into the street and are almost trampled by a giant papier-mâché puppet because now we're running through the Halloween parade. I look behind us and see the men from the park.

I wake up standing naked in the dark of my room, the towel from my shower on the floor, my fists clenched, my body tense. I am screaming her name.

I remember.

Seemy, I am coming for you.

REMEMBERING YESTERDAY

"This is Nanja!" Seemy said, taking hold of my hand and tugging me toward the two men sitting on the back of our favorite little blue bench. She pointed at the men, her breath coming out in excited huffs. "That's Turner, and the other one we call Hooch." She giggled nervously, swung my hand like we were little kids. "So . . . that's who they are."

"Hey," they said in unison. I looked at them, and the bottom dropped out from my stomach. They were a couple of randoms, sketchy-looking men with dead eyes and sunken cheeks and unshaven faces. Suddenly the tiny little park felt too small, and I looked through the gate and saw that the sidewalks were filling with parents and kids in costumes, out trick-or-treating before dark, and I wished I had said yes when my dad asked if I wanted to come out to Greenpoint and go trick-or-treating with him and the Tick.

I looked at Seemy, seeing if she was joking about their very fake-sounding names, and I saw maybe she didn't look exactly the same. She looked thin, washed out. She made me think of the word "sinew." Her eyes had grown, or her face had shrunk, I wasn't sure which one. Her pupils looked too big for her eyes. I wondered what she had taken. I wondered how long it would last. I could feel the tiny bones in her freezing cold hand as she squeezed.

I wanted to get out of there. And I wanted to take Seemy with me.

I could have just started walking, pulled her with me. Turner and Hooch were watching me, like they knew what I was thinking, like they knew what I was going to do. The sound of my heart thump-thump-thumped in my ears and I made myself look right back at them. *I'm not afraid of you,* I thought, and it's like I said it out loud, because both of them wrinkled their mouths into ugly smirks.

I was about to say something to Seemy, about to walk and pull her with me, about to tell those assholes that if they touched us, I would scream bloody murder. Seemy nudged me. She was holding a half-empty soda bottle. "Sip?"

"I don't drink anymore," I said quietly, my eyes still on Turner and Hooch. "You know that."

"It's just soda. Vanilla Coke. Your favorite." She nudged me again, and when I looked at her, she looked so hurt I took it from her and took a drink.

"Thought you was calling a friend," the one called Turner said.

"I did! This is Nanja!" Seemy wrapped her skinny arms around my waist. "My best, best friend. We *always* hang out on Halloween together."

"She's your friend?" Hooch asked. Then he and Turner looked at each other and started laughing, low grumbly wet laughs. "Looks more like your bodyguard."

"We thought you was calling a *hot* friend," Turner said. "We thought it was going to be a party."

"But I told you, silly, I already have plans!" Seemy laughed. She wagged a finger at him like he was a naughty child, giving me a desperate sideways glance. "I always spend Halloween with my Nan!"

She was afraid. My pulse quickened and I did my best to grin, slinging an arm around her. Her shoulder bones poked into my forearm. "Are you ready?" I asked her. I started to turn her around, barely glancing at Turner and Hooch. "We have friends waiting," I told them.

With our backs turned, I whispered, "Let's go, Seemy. Just walk."

I tried to move her forward, but she stood firm. She looked up at me. "They won't let me leave."

I glanced back, saw them both stand slowly, watching us.

"What do you mean they won't let you leave?" I whispered. "You can just walk away. Watch, like this."

I took a step, pulled her with me.

"Hey." Turner moved fast off the bench, stepping in front of us. "Where you going? Thought we were all going to party."

"She's partied enough," I answered, trying to move around him, glancing behind me to see Hooch still sitting on the bench, head tipped to the side, watching.

"Not nearly." I think he was trying to chuckle, but it came out a dry rasp. "She's just getting started."

"We're leaving," I told him. He stepped in front of me again. Bastard. I had an inch and at least ten pounds on him. I imagined cracking my fist against his chin. I was scared to hit him, though. I didn't want him to hit me back. So instead I asked, "You want to hear me scream?"

He gave a half smile. "Kind of."

It took me a second to realize Seemy was pulling away. "Relax, Nanja," she said nervously. "We're all just going to hang out for a while, then we can leave. Right?" She directed the question at Turner.

He nodded. "Sure, we'll just all hang out for a little while and then you can leave."

"Seemy." I tried to step closer to her, so I could lower my voice and speak without them hearing. She took a step back. "Seemy," I said again, stepping forward. She stood on her tiptoes, pulled on my arm so I bent over, and then whispered in my ear. "They'll find us." I pulled back, looked at her. Her lower lip quivered. "I'm sorry," she whispered. "I'm so sorry."

Then she stepped away. "Come on, Nan," she said. "Come out with us for a while. It'll be fun."

"What's wrong with your eyes?" I asked, leaning in to stare into her face. Her eyes were almost all pupil now, black holes in her head.

Seemy looked at Turner, and Turner looked back at Hooch, and the two men laughed.

"Guess it kicked in." Turner said.

"What kicked in?" I asked.

"Liquid Gold." He cackled, wiggling his fingers at me like he was casting a spell.

I grabbed Seemy's chin and looked into her eyes again, letting go as Seemy pulled free. She glared at the two men. "You told me it was just vodka."

"What'd you give her?" I demanded, stepping up to Turner.

He laughed. "Told you. Liquid Gold."

"I don't know what that is," I snapped.

"You'll find out!" He cackled again.

"What do you mean?" He didn't answer, he just looked at Seemy. "Seemy?" My heart started pounding. "What does he mean?"

Her chin dropped and I heard her sniff. "They said it was just vodka." She held up the Vanilla Coke bottle. "I'm not . . . I'm not thinking right."

"You dosed me?" I yelled. "What the hell, Seemy?"

Turner and Hooch cracked up laughing. I glared at Seemy. As angry as I was, I wasn't going to leave her there. "Seemy, come on," I said, taking her arm, "let's go. We have to go."

But then something went wrong with my brain. I felt it. I could feel it changing. I could feel something like cold syrup seeping in and I was watching Seemy and she was watching me and I said again, "We have to go." But I think my voice might have sounded weird, now because Turner and Hooch kept cracking up. Turner said, "We have to go!"

And then we were walking out of the park and . . .

Darkness. Like the space between pictures in a slide show. It was just for a moment.

And when the show started again, we were walking with them even though we didn't want to be and even though I wanted to run away. But Seemy had her arm through mine, and I didn't know if I could get her to run away too and my body felt so strange and my head hurt so much and I didn't know how I would do anything ever again.

We were walking and walking down sidewalks crowded with people in costumes. Turner and Hooch were on either side of us. Bookends. Or jailers. They wanted us to go with them somewhere. I kept blacking out. A minute. Maybe five.

Darkness.

They kept making us turn corners.

Darkness.

First they said we were going to Turner's apartment, and then they said to a friend's place, and then they said they had a room at a hotel right in Times Square.

Darkness.

Everyone and everything I looked at was swimming and swaying and jerking and twitching. It was getting dark out, and the streetlights and the store lights and the apartment lights were all pulsing out different rhythms.

Darkness.

We were walking for a long time and Turner or maybe Hooch said, "We're almost there," and then all of a sudden

Seemy said, "We need costumes!" and she ran in front of Turner and pulled me with her. We ran into Ricky's, and even though there was a line out the door, she just cut right to the front. She turned around quickly, held up her hands to push back on Turner's chest. "Wait outside," she ordered. "Our costumes are a surprise!"

Darkness.

I was in the dressing room with Seemy. The dressing room was tiny, just enough room for a little leopard-print-covered stool and a mirror on the wall. She held two pink dresses. There wasn't a door to the dressing room, just a vinyl curtain decorated with hula girls that ended a foot away from the floor. I pressed my back flat against the wall, a wave of dizziness threatening to knock me over. I let myself slide down until I was sitting on the little stool and held my head in my hands. "I keep losing time, Seemy. I keep blacking out."

"I know. Me too," she said, nudging my arms out of the way with her hip and sitting on my lap. She dropped the dresses on the floor. And then we were looking at each other in the mirror and it was so familiar, the way we looked together. She was so small, and I was like her dark shadow sitting behind her.

I wrapped my arms around her waist and buried my face in her back. Darkness.

"We have to get away from them," Seemy said. I could feel the vibrations of her voice against the bridge of my nose. I moved my head so I could rest my chin on her shoulder. "I know," she whispered. "I have a plan. I'm going to save us."

But then she just went real still, and even though she was looking at me in the mirror, I could see she couldn't see me. I could feel myself slipping into darkness and I shook my head hard to wake up, and the movement jostled Seemy back into herself.

"I'm going to save us," she said again.

"Come on out!" We looked down and saw Turner's boots at the bottom of the curtain. "We want to see."

"Hold on!" I called to him. "We just need a different size."

"I told you!" Seemy slipped off my lap and stuck her head out of the dressing room to say to Turner, "You have to go wait outside." Turner grumbled, and Seemy said, "It will be worth it, promise!"

She pulled back into the dressing room and squeezed my hand as we watched his boots under the curtain. They stayed put for a moment, and then they were gone. Seemy held up her hand, counting down from five on pale fingers, then she stuck her head out of the dressing room for a second. "He's gone," she said breathlessly.

Darkness.

"Nan! I said he's gone." Seemy was next to me, shaking my shoulder.

"Let's call the police," I said.

She shook her head frantically. "No cops!"

"But why, Seemy?" Something about what she said didn't make sense, but I couldn't make my brain figure out the thoughts I was trying to think. "Why no cops?"

"Because." Her eyes went even wider. "Turner and Hooch . . . they have something on me." She poked her head out of the dressing room for a second again. Then she leaned close to my ear and whispered with sour breath, "I've been doing bad things, Nan. I could go to jail."

She nodded off then, standing up, her eyes this time rolling back into her head, her mouth dropping open. I caught her as she fell, sat her down on the stool. She opened up her eyes, stood back up, and picked up the dresses off the floor. "We have to hurry before they come back inside. Come on. Get dressed."

I looked at the dresses. "But we haven't paid for these yet."

She wrinkles her brow. "I did, Nan. You were standing right next to me. We have to hurry!" she whispered urgently, wiggling out of her clothes. I felt my jaw go loose at the sight of her shrunken body. She stepped into one of the dresses and yanked it up, spinning around so I could zip her up. Her back looked even worse than her front.

Darkness.

"Nan, please!"

She was shaking me again. I zipped her up slowly; her body looked so brittle I didn't want her to crack.

"Now you!" she said, holding out the other dress. I looked at the tag. It was a size small. "The lady says there are no larger sizes. I'll help you get it on. Come on."

She had to stand on the stool to get enough leverage to yank the dress up, and she could barely get it to zip. As soon as I took a breath, it split a little down the side, but at least that made it easier to breathe.

"We have to hurry," Seemy said, reaching into her pants on the floor and pulling out a jar of white face paint she'd lifted from the store. She opened it and stuck her fingers in and held my chin still with her other hand, quickly smearing the paint all over my face. She looked at our reflections in the mirror, and I finally figured out what her plan was.

"You can still tell it's me," I said, and her eyes filled with tears. "Hold on." I got my black Sharpie out of my backpack. "Use this for the eyes and mouth."

She nodded and pushed my hair back away from my face, rested her hand against my face as she drew. The fumes stung my eyes, made my nose run. She circled my eyes over and over again, making the skeleton eyeholes go all the way down to my cheeks. She pressed the pen hard on my mouth, scribbling back and forth and back again. When she was done, I looked terrible, like a lunatic clown, but I still looked like myself.

"We have to cut off your hair," she said. "They'll know it's you."

Darkness.

She was walking into the dressing room with scissors. It hurt because my hair is so thick that she half cut, half sawed it off. It fell in loose ropes to the dressing-room floor, tickled my bare legs. We stuffed the hair into my backpack along with my clothes, and then I did her makeup. We left her hair because it was so short anyway. "We'll take wigs on the way out," Seemy said. "We should go. Put on your shoes."

First I got out my pen and wrote a message on the wall. Because I didn't know if Seemy could save us. I didn't know if anyone could.

We heard Turner's gravelly voice cut through the noise in the crowded store. "Samanthaaaa . . . where are yoooou?"

Seemy grabbed my hand. "We have to go. We have to stay awake."

"But our clothes . . ."

She kicked my backpack under the stool and peeked out the curtain. "We'll come back for it," she said.

Darkness.

We were running through the store and knocking into people and displays and racks of costumes and we burst out the front door and knocked right into Hooch.

Turner came out with my backpack and our shoes. He said he saw our little note.

They made sure to hold on to us after that.

Turner was mad, but Hooch thought it was funny.

They gave us some more to drink.

Darkness.

They said we were going to a hotel. We were trying to find their car.

But then I heard myself say I was hungry. And Seemy said she was too. And Turner said, "We'll order room service."

Darkness.

But then we were at Duke's and I didn't know how we got there. It felt like there was a black curtain hanging halfway down my eyeballs, and even though I kept tilting my head up, I couldn't see.

I was in the bathroom with Seemy and we were trying to get off the face paint. I was crying about my hair. Some girl tried to help with the paint, but the wet cloth she gave me smelled like floor cleaner and it made me gag. Seemy said, "We should try to run again." And she had to say it a few times before I could find my tongue to say, "Yes."

We were going to run right then, but we were scared to run by the table where Turner and Hooch were sitting. So we sat with them. And then Edie made us leave. I wanted to grab on to her legs and start screaming, but I couldn't make my body do what I wanted to.

Darkness.

We were in a car. It smelled musty, and like engine oil. Turner and Hooch took our shoes. I said I was going to be sick. Turner rolled down my window. I hung my head out. It was a blue car. I reached back with one hand and did *One, two, three* with my fingers and then Seemy pushed me out of the window and climbed out after me. My backpack thumped against me as we ran. It was lucky we were in my neighborhood, because we snuck by the night doorman, went to my apartment, and hid in the bathroom for a while.

Seemy's phone rang, and when she picked up, she looked at me so scared.

Darkness.

We were on the street again. We were running. Seemy said Turner and Hooch knew where I lived now. They had followed us, but we got away from them.

Darkness.

They were right behind us. We ran across the street, through the parade. Turner was fast. He grabbed Seemy, but she reached out and grabbed my arm, digging her nails into my skin, scraping down from the elbow to my wrist. I pulled her away from him, ran between the legs of a puppet and into the crowd.

The darkness was lasting longer now. I could feel myself being stuck inside of it, drowning in it, clawing to get out.

It looked like we had lost them. And then I was pulling Seemy down the alley to the carriage house, and for a second I was so scared it was like I flew up out of myself and watched us from above: bare feet, pink dresses, eyes too big for our heads, our bare arms and legs stretching out like spider limbs as I pushed Seemy up over the gate.

The yard was wet, the mud squished between our toes and over our feet. I stepped on something sharp and cried out.

Darkness.

We were upstairs in the carriage house, in the back hayloft, pressed into the storage closet. Seemy's heart was thumping against my chest.

"They'll find us, Nan," she whispered.

"No they won't," I told her. "This is our place, remember? They won't find us here."

Seemy's knees buckled and I caught her under her arms. I had to open the closet door so I could lay her down. Her eyes were open, her eyelids twitched.

I stood so I could see out the hole in the wall where the window used to be. The front yard and alley were empty, but I was terrified Turner and Hooch would find us here.

I knelt next to her. "Seemy, you have to get up. We have to be ready to run."

She stared at me, unseeing for a moment, and then blinked and focused. "It keeps getting dark in my eyes, Nan."

"I know, me too."

"I want it to stay light."

"It will. You just have to sit up."

Her eyes went blank again. I waved my hands in front of her face, but she wouldn't even blink. It was a full minute before she came to. "I'm so tired, Nan." she said. "I'm just going to lay here for a while."

"I'm going to go get help," I told her.

She didn't answer.

"Seemy," I said, shaking her shoulder. It took a moment, but her eyes focused on mine.

"You'll forget me," she said.

"I would never forget you." I stood up. "I'm coming back for you."

"No," she said. And she sounded so sad. "That's part of it. What they gave us. It makes you forget things. You're going to forget. And they're going to find me."

I took the Sharpie out of my backpack.

"Don't let me forget," I told her, kneeling down again. She wrote hard on my chest.

"Come back for me," she said.

"I won't forget," I promised. "I won't forget."

Darkness.

I woke up watching. There was a spilled cup of coffee under a subway seat. *Oh man*, I thought, *all that coffee. And it looks nice and creamy, too. Probably lots of sugar. Someone's good morning, just dumped out. That sucks.*

TODAY

CHAPTER 27

I am running through the rain in the night. The water soaks through the hood of my sweatshirt and runs down my head, my neck, my back.

I say her name to the rhythm of my wet steps. "Seemy, Seemy, Seemy."

I take a side street that is empty except for a car that I can hear chugging along behind me, but it never passes. It coughs, like a dying thing.

And then I am tearing down the alley to the carriage house, scrambling over the fence, across the muddy front lawn, and up the warped front steps. "Seemy Seemy Seemy." Inside I scramble up the ladder to the hayloft.

The storage closet door is closed, and I run to it but don't open it up.

I close my eyes, and pray her name. "Seemy Seemy Seemy."

I open the door.

She lies crumpled on the floor, her body bent to fit the confines of the closet. I drop to my knees and with one hand cover my mouth and nose from the stench and with the other lay my fingers against her neck. Her blood pulses my name. *Nan, Nan, Nan.*

She is alive.

"Seemy." My tears make it sound like I am swallowing the word, so I say it louder, "Seemy!"

Her eyes stay closed.

A car drives down the street outside, *chug, chug, chug.* It doesn't pass by the alley. It stops and idles. *Chug, chug, chug.* I stand up and go to the window but can see nothing in the dark. *Chug, chug, chug.* Like a cough. Like a dying thing. Like the car behind me earlier today on the way to bring Chuck his pizza, and then on the way from Duke's to Saint Marks. Like the car that drove behind me all the way here.

I look down at Seemy and cover my mouth to keep from screaming.

I led them right to her.

—

It's too small in the closet. Too dark. I stand awkwardly with one foot by Seemy's knee, the other by her head. My right hand holds the door shut against the weight of Seemy's body.

I can hear the car still chugging on the street.

There is a click and a creak as the barn-style doors are shoved apart. Footsteps on the stone floor. The creak of stall doors as they are pulled open one by one.

Turner's gravelly voice, a sick singsong calling out, "Oh, girls, I'm home!"

I stay still, blinking away the sweat that is pooling in the corners of my eyes. I stay still except for my eyes. They move with each step he takes across the first floor, like I am watching him instead of staring into the dark.

He calls out as he walks. "Are you in the first stall? Hooch has the car all warmed up for you." There is the sound of the doors being kicked open. "No, not in that one."

"Are you in the second stall?" I hear the groan of the stall door. "No, not in that one either."

He does this for each stall. "Well," he says loudly, "I guess nobody's home."

I know he's screwing with us. I know he knows I can hear him. I hear the front door squeak. "I guess I'll just go, then."

He doesn't even finish the sentence before he scrambles

up the ladder. Every drop of blood in my body is screaming at me to run. But I don't. I stay still. My hand on the
doorknob is cramping. I squeeze the knob harder to keep
from shaking.

Mom says bodies like ours are made to cast large shad-
ows. She says we're meant to lift the world up on our shoulders and spin it round. She says we're meant to roar through
our lives and kick up dust.

He is in the hayloft with us now. He is walking quickly
across the floor.

My fingers wrench as the doorknob is turned.

I hold on to the door, and Turner pulls harder. I hold
on for a moment and then just as he starts to rasp, "Come
out, come out, wherever you are," I slam myself against
the door so that it crashes open, and then I am tumbling
with Turner across the room. It strikes me then how horribly intimate fighting someone is. I can smell him, feel his
breath on my face as he grunts, feel the texture of his palm
as it grips the curve where my neck and shoulder meet, feel
his other hand in a fist, gripping the fabric of my sweatshirt, pulling me close to him until we are chest to chest.
He twists both hands; I realize he's trying to push me off
balance, and I struggle to stay upright. I'm surprised at
his strength, scared of how solid he feels, terrified of feeling his weight on top of me. His laugh is dry and gleeful,

and I fight to stay standing, until he kicks my feet out from under me. I land hard on the floor, my right hip and elbow taking most of the weight of my fall. It *hurts*.

But my body is my battleship, and I will not be sunk. I kick up, hard, right between his legs and then roll away as he doubles over, his arms shooting out to grab me. I scramble up to my feet.

Turner tries to stand up straight, but I've hurt him and he has to hunch. He's ten feet away. We both sway a little, waiting for the other to move. There is quietness in fighting for your life. There are only the sounds of our feet on the dusty floor, of our breathing, of our clothing rubbing against itself. Turner breaks the silence. "Big girl's got a big kick," he says.

I don't answer. I just watch him, my body tense and ready to move. I vibrate with fear and adrenaline and the realization that comes again and again: This is really happening. I want to scream for help, but I'm afraid Hooch will hear. I can't fight them both.

"How's little Samantha?" Turner asks, looking past me to where Seemy lies half in and half out of the closet. He moves a little closer. I step back, closer to the closet, my body shaking in expectation. "How's she feeling right now?" He steps to his right, forcing me to step away. "Because I'd guess she has just a couple more hours until it's lights-out."

He moves again, and I have to move too, and then our positions are reversed and he is by the closet door, between me and Seemy. He keeps talking. "We might have gave her too much. But that girl can *drink*! You know that, right? You, though, you and your little sips, it'll take longer for you."

I need to keep him talking, I need to keep him from turning his attention to Seemy. I ask him, "What do you mean?"

His laugh is almost soundless now, a wet rush of air. "You been walking around dead all day and you don't even know it!"

Behind him, Seemy stirs a little.

I can't help it, I look at her face, and while my eyes aren't on him, Turner says, "I'm just going to have to speed it up for both y'all." And then he lunges at me. I force myself not to move and let him grab my shoulders. I put my hands on top of his, grip hard, and spin hard to the right, yanking him off balance. I keep spinning and then let go, hoping he will fly across the floor. He doesn't. He stumbles only a few steps, but when he looks at me he doesn't look like he's having fun anymore. He looks pissed. He recovers fast, raises a fist, and comes at me again, but this time I move so he runs right at the empty window frame. He stops short, turns and spits at me. "Clever girl, but I ain't going out the window."

He comes at me again and there are sounds of footsteps coming up the front steps and into the house. My heart drops and Turner sneers at me in triumph. "Up here!" he yells, and I know in a minute Hooch is going to come scrambling up the ladder and I'm going to have to fight them both, and I'm probably going to lose. I look at Seemy, lying still on the floor, and I'm filled with such sadness. And more than that. Bubbling up through the sadness, snaking up and breaking the surface, is rage. *Anger is a gift.* My body bursts into flames. It doesn't matter that Turner can't see them. I am on fire.

He's surprised when I grab on to his wrists, and I can see him trying to figure out what I'm doing. I can see him for the first time feeling *my* weight, *my* strength, *my* power. I wrench him forward and he laughs, moving his feet fast to keep from falling over. I yank harder this time, swinging him a little, and he's caught off guard, so this time he leans back, trying to pull me off balance. For a moment we are suspended like that, holding each other up. And then I let go. He falls against the windowsill and as I'm dropping to my knees he gives me this look like, *Nice try.* I grab both of his feet, pull them up off the floor, and flip that monster out the window.

I turn just as the top rung of the ladder creaks.

I am ready to fight again.

But I don't have to.

Toad bursts into the room, fists raised in an almost comic stance. He screams, "Where is she?"

"What . . . what are you doing here?" I shout, all of the breath and fire in my body escaping. I am so relieved to see his stupid face I could cry. "What are you doing here?" I ask again.

"Saving Seemy!" he says, looking around wildly.

I can't even speak; I just point to the window.

He walks over uncertainly, and we both look outside. Below, Turner's pale face glints in the moonlight. He landed on his back, the soft mud sucking him in so his arms and legs stick up a little, like a roach stuck on its back. He moves one arm a little and then his howl of pain travels up to us. Toad leans out and spits on him. The front yard is lit up then. First by police car lights reflecting down the narrow alley, and then by flashlights sweeping across the front lawn. We watch one light settle on Turner and grow more intense as the police officer approaches and leans over him. She calls into the radio on her shoulder for an ambulance. Another beam of light travels up to where we stand in the window. We both raise a hand, shielding our eyes, and back away.

I hurry over to Seemy and drop to my knees.

"I came here and looked for her. Before, I mean. Before

you came to see me." Toad says, staying by the window. I glance at him. He looks terrified. His words rush out. "I swear it, Nan. I came here and I called out for her. I checked the stalls. But I didn't come up here. I don't know why I didn't think of it. I just . . . I should have come up here. And then after I saw you, I remembered. Like, like, flash. Boom! I remembered the hayloft . . ." He trails off, raises his chin and asks with a quivering voice, "Is she dead?"

I shake my head, almost smile. "No, she's not dead."

He walks over, drops to the floor next to me. We each take one of her hands. I can hear the carriage house doors being pushed all the way open.

"Are you okay?" he asks me.

I shake my head, the darkness creeping in. "Tell them to help Seemy. Tell them to help her."

Toad looks at me. "What'd they give you?"

Darkness.

EPILOGUE

I dream about Seemy sometimes.

We're at her parents' farm, and we're walking through a cornfield in the sun, like we're in a laundry detergent commercial or something. There are corn plants between us, towering higher than our heads, filtering the sunlight, and I can't get a clear view of her. I catch glimpses of her hair. Her narrow wrist. Her pointed chin. I hear her laugh my name. I reach out to take her hand, I want to pull her toward me so I can see her face. But she's too far away, even though she's right next to me.

I wake up and have to remind myself she's not dead.

She's just in a room somewhere with locks on the windows but no lock on the bathroom door. I get this desperate need sometimes to know if she can see the sky from her room. I asked Mom about it once and she said, "She's at a boarding school rehab for rich kids, dollface, not solitary confinement. I'm sure if it wasn't there already, her parents had the sky imported."

It took them two days to suck the poison out of me. Two days I spent dreaming that I was digging my way out of a sleep that pressed itself against me from all sides—a thick, rich, black soil. I woke exhausted, my arms and legs spent from dreamed effort.

I could only stay awake for a moment at first, but the sight of Mom and Dad and the Tick by my bedside made being sucked under not as scary. I knew they would be waiting for me when I dug my way out again.

When I woke up for real Mom told me not to cry and wiped away my tears with her fingertips. I kept saying, *I'm sorry, I'm sorry, I'm sorry*, and she kept saying, *I know, my love, I know*. Dad was holding the Tick; I said to the Tick, *Hey buddy*, and he hid his face in Dad's shoulder. Dad bent down to kiss me on the forehead, and the Tick practically coiled himself around Dad's neck so we wouldn't have to touch.

It was Thanksgiving before he would let me hug him

again. At first I thought he was just angry at me. But then in family therapy it came out that he was actually afraid to love me, because it would hurt too much when I died again. Not *if*, but *when*. Hearing that felt like a punch in the throat. It's amazing how much love and anger and fear can fit in one little kid's body.

It's cold now, almost Christmas, and most mornings I wake up with the Tick curled up beside me, hugging my arm like a teddy bear, holding tight to make sure I don't go anywhere. It was Dr. Friedman who found us the family therapist, and besides the family therapy and the just me therapy, Mom and I go to see her, just the two of us. I never saw Mom looking like she wanted to fold up into herself until I sat across from her in the therapist's office. I'd never seen her not relish the structure of her bones or solidness of her body. She looked as though she wanted to slide between the cushions like a lost penny.

Therapy is a lot of talking and "active listening." Sometimes it's kind of amazing and sometimes it's kind of exhausting. It's helping, though. I know that, because it doesn't hurt to look at Mom anymore, and I don't think it hurts her to look at me. We still fight. About my hair, mostly, since I shaved it into a Mohawk when I got out of the hospital. I'm hoping it will be long enough to have liberty spikes by the time summer comes. Truth is, we both kind of enjoy bickering about my hair. It feels so normal.

I see Dad a lot more now. I go out to Greenpoint Sunday mornings and spend the day with him and the Tick, and then bring the Tick home Sunday night. Mom doesn't come. I know it bothers the Tick, and it bothers me, but I told him you can't make people love each other. It's going to have to be enough that he and I love Mom and Dad, and that they love us.

Toad and I hung out the other night. Weird, right? I asked Mom for permission first. Toad wasn't worth getting in trouble over. She said he had to come up to our apartment first, and by the time she was done grilling him (and feeding him milk and cookies because he was *too damn skinny*) it was dark out. Hearing her ask him questions I learned all sorts of things. Like, Toad actually has a family. They live in New Jersey. He never stopped living with them and would go home every night after hanging out with Seemy and me. I always assumed he slept in some crappy, rat-infested flophouse. The ugly truth is that's what I wanted to believe. He graduated in May and is in school now, at CUNY, for graphic design.

We walked up to Union Square and looked at the Christmas lights. He bought me a hot apple cider. We talked about a lot of stuff. He said he was glad I didn't drink anymore, because I was a spectacularly bad drunk. He could tell I never enjoyed it. We laughed at that for a while. He said he liked my hair, especially since I wasn't pairing it with *all that weird black clothing* anymore. He said I used to look like the Grim Reaper. I tensed up a little, worried he would tell me I looked stupid wearing the sort of things Seemy used to wear, except not quite as twee. I like having a Mohawk and wearing a red party dress with my lace-up combat boots. But he didn't say anything bad. We talked about Seemy. Of course. *I hated you,* he said, *because she loved you. Maybe not the way you wanted. But she did. She loved you.* I smiled at him. *Yeah, well. Right back at you.* I think we were both bummed to learn that she hadn't contacted either of us.

Without either of us acknowledging it, we walked up to the carriage house. On the way we compared what information we had about Turner and Hooch.

They are in jail, awaiting trial. They thought they'd hit a gold mine when they met Seemy in the park on Halloween. They had all sorts of plans for her.

When we got to the alley that leads to the carriage house we stopped and didn't walk any further. We looked down the alley and saw they've built a plywood fence, blocking any view. Neither of us said anything for a long time. Finally I said, *She loved this place.* Toad smiled, snorted. *I knew she would. Didn't matter though.* I shook my head, *No, I guess it didn't.* He looked at me, a bemused expression on his face. *What do you think it says about us? That we spent so much time trying to get her to love us the way we wanted her to?* I shrugged. *Self-esteem issues? I don't know. That's what my therapist thinks, anyway. For you,* I said with a smile, *it just means you're a shmuck.* He knocked me lightly in the shoulder. We looked down the alley for another moment, and then it just seemed obvious that it was time to say good-bye. Toad nodded at me. *See you around.* I nodded back. *Maybe.* I think we both knew it was a lie.

I'm still going to my new school. Kids saw what happened to me, what almost happened to me, on the news, so my anonymity is gone. It's okay, though. The stoic lone wolf thing kind of sucked.

Mom says I'll get through this. She says everyone has a tough time when they're a teenager. Sometimes, I even believe her. I can go whole hours, days, and once even a whole weekend without my body going rigid with memory—and even worse, flashes of what might have been. I feel these flashes of false memory as if they were real, as if I were a ghost unable to shake the violence of my death. When I feel this way I trace the four thin white scars from my elbow to my wrist and rest my fingers on my pulse with its reassuring rhythm. *Still Here. Still Here. Still Here.*

ACKNOWLEDGMENTS

My deepest thanks to Tracey Adams for making my dreams come true, to Karen Wojtyla for her patience and insight as Nan's story morphed from one thing to another and back again, and to Emily Fabre for her good humor and for asking difficult questions. Thank you to my mom and dad and big brother, to all of my aunties and uncles and cousins, and to all of my family north and south. Thank you to my family at 557 Broadway. And thank you to the Brooklyn coffee houses that gave me a place to scribble away: Champion Coffee, the Greenpoint Coffee House, and Brooklyn Label.